TIME OF DEATH

A DI FRANK MILLER NOVEL

JOHN CARSON

DI FRANK MILLER SERIES

Crash Point
Silent Marker
Rain Town
Watch Me Bleed
Broken Wheels
Sudden Death
Under the Knife
Trial and Error
Warning Sign
Cut Throat
Blood from a Stone
Time of Death

Frank Miller Crime Series – Books 1-3 – Box set
Frank Miller Crime Series - Books 4-6 - Box set

MAX DOYLE SERIES

SCOTT MARSHALL SERIES

Old Habits

TIME OF DEATH

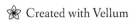

For Michael Salamin

ONE

Andy Watt stood six feet away from the stone-cold killer and didn't blink.

'She doesn't know you're here,' Jill White said. The psychologist put her hand on Watt's arm.

'Neither do Professional Standards.'

'I won't tell them if you won't.'

He looked through the one-way mirror into the room where Dr Eve Ross sat. Her other personality, the deadly one, was being kept at bay by the meds. The drugs coursing through her system kept her on the right track. This was the woman he had known, not the psychopathic one who had tried to kill him.

'She's a nice woman, and nobody knew she had a killer lurking inside of her,' he said, turning away from the woman who was sitting talking to a psychiatrist. Jill worked between here, the Royal Scottish psychiatric hospital and the Astley Ainslie clinic across the road in Morningside.

'She'll never stand trial. She'll spend the rest of her life here.'

Watt looked at her. 'Now that she's back on her meds, she'll wonder why she can't go home.'

'That's the transition part. We'll take good care of her, Andy, don't worry.'

They turned out of the small observation room and walked along the corridor. 'That's the thing, doc; I *do* worry. If I hadn't met her, she would have still been working in Langholm.'

They stopped at the lift doors. 'Langholm was the last chance saloon for her. You told me they found journals written by Simon Larking, the murdered professor. The one who Eve killed when her personality was Angel. He had told Eve that this was her last chance. He couldn't keep covering for her. Everything was going smoothly, but she'd only been there a few months. I personally think she would have snapped eventually.'

The lift doors opened and they stepped inside.

'I was the one who gave her the final push,' Watt said as the doors slid shut.

'Listen, the drugs kept her straight, but she didn't want that life. She chose not to take them, knowing what would happen when she came off them. She chose to come looking for you, but Angel had taken her over completely by then. There was never any chance of a real relationship. You can't blame yourself for this, Andy.'

He nodded as the lift went down to the ground floor.

The hospital was quiet. The rain had stopped now but it was cold. Halloween was a couple of weeks away. A couple more months and he'd be a grandad. And he'd be celebrating his fifty-first birthday next week.

Jill buttoned her coat up. 'Can I give you a lift anywhere?'

'Thanks, doc, but I'm meeting somebody.'

She smiled. 'I hope she cheers you up.'

'How do you know it's a *she*?'

'I'm a woman, Andy.'

'How do you all do that?' he said as they walked towards the exit. They passed through security and went outside into the damp, dark evening.

'Take care of yourself, Andy, and you know where my office is. Just call ahead and I'll make time for you.'

'Thanks, Jill.'

He watched her back as she walked over to the small red car and got in. He waved as she drove past him. He thought she was a remarkable woman; her little boy had been kidnapped and had been found years later, dead. She had gone to the brink and back and seemed to be leading a normal life. He didn't know how he himself would have handled losing a child.

His thoughts turned to his daughters, both of them happily married, one of them expecting, and he tried to focus on that instead of Eve Ross.

He hardly took notice of the Audi as it pulled up in front of the doors. Then the passenger side window rolled down. 'Are you going to get in?'

He smiled and got in the passenger seat. 'You're a bit lippy for an Uber driver,' he said, putting his seat belt on.

'If I was an Uber driver, I'd boot your arse to the kerb,' Kate Murphy said, her London accent sounding strong.

'Dearie me, what kind of profanity is that? And you a doctor, too.' He smiled, leaned over, and kissed her.

'Oh wow, I'm impressed. First holding hands in public, then kissing me in my car. You'll be asking me to get in the back seat next.'

'Listen, if my back could put up with it, I'd show you a good time.'

'You can show me a good time by taking me to dinner. The Merlin is just round the corner. Then we can go back to my place.'

She drove slowly out of the hospital car park and followed the roads round to Morningside Road.

'Do you think we could just pick up a Chinese and eat at your flat?'

'Of course we can. As long as you aren't going to try and take advantage of me afterwards.'

'You know me, doc; not on a full stomach.'

They picked up the meal at their usual takeaway, and Kate parked in the underground car park at her building on Holyrood Road.

They joked around before dishing the food out. Then when Kate had poured the wine and lit a candle, she looked across at Watt.

'You said you were going to give me an answer tonight,' she said, forking some food into her mouth.

'Okay, you got me. I was putting it off but I'll give you a straight answer; I've never actually played golf before.'

'Okay, we've been seeing more of each other the past few months. Then we moved on from policeman having a drink with the pathologist. Now we're dating, and I asked you if you would like to move in with me.'

He ate some food and avoided eye contact for a moment before looking past the tall candle directly at her.

'And I said I'd think about it. And I have.'

'Well? Don't keep me in suspense.'

Watt took a drink of the wine. 'The situation is, as you know, I've been crashing at Paddy's place. Which he's been great about, and Maggie Parks too. They haven't been rushing me to get out but I know that I need to look for my own place. However, I don't want people to think I'm just moving in with you because I don't have my own place.'

'I don't care what people think, Andy. *I* know you would be doing it for the right reason. We *both* know it.'

He nodded and put his glass down. 'Let me just mull it over a little bit more. I promise I won't keep you hanging. It's just got to feel right inside.'

'I understand. I don't want to pressure you.' She got up and came round the table, put her arms round his shoulders and leaned over to kiss him.

'I love you, Andy Watt.'

'I love you, too, Kate.'

TWO

'I wish you hadn't brought him along,' Cara Robertson said, turning and making a face at her brother.

'Relax. He knows we're the team behind the YouTube channel. He's just a gopher. Besides, you should have seen him; he was so excited when he knew we were coming here.'

Ben shone the torch around the cold, damp nuclear bunker under Corstorphine Hill. Josh was a friend they'd brought along with them, although the other man didn't have anything to do with their videos. Ben felt sorry for him. 'I can't imagine so many politicians under one roof if the big bomb had gone off.'

'They'd be falling over each other to get in.' Cara made a face. 'As long as the public weren't allowed in, eh?'

Neither Ben nor his sister worked. They were in

their twenties and living off their video channel. They roamed the UK filming abandoned buildings and were about to expand into America. First though, they were going to explore the bunker where the great minds of Edinburgh and beyond would have raced to had Russia decided to fire off a nuke.

Their friend and co-host, Marty Williams, came up behind them. 'You two old wifies ready to start rolling? Time is of the essence. Filmed, edited, and uploaded by tomorrow. Then we have a plane to catch.'

'It's not like we have to worry about the sun going down. Considering we're in the bowels of hell,' Cara said, shivering. 'We should have done this in summer.'

'It wouldn't have been warmer in here, dozy cow,' Marty said, laughing.

'Shut up.'

They walked further in. Josh had run ahead and they couldn't see him anymore.

'I told you, he's like a kid you can't take your eyes off,' Cara moaned as her own light shone around the cold concrete walls.

They were in a narrow corridor with a set of steps ahead of them. Josh was out of sight.

'I'm telling you, if there's something amiss in here, I'm off,' Marty said. 'You can stay behind and look for him if you want, but I'm not. I'll call for help from outside, of course.'

'Wanker,' Cara said.

'Every man for himself when push comes to shove.'

'Will you two shut up and concentrate. I'm about to start filming.'

They walked up the concrete steps and the corridor was short, turning round to the left. They each shone their lights and could hear banging from ahead.

Ben was in the lead, talking about the bunker.

'I hope he's not playing around with electrical wires,' Marty whispered.

'Serve him right,' Cara said. 'Kentucky Fried Josh. Except nobody would want to lick their fingers after touching the boggin' bastard.'

'Ease up. Josh doesn't get out much,' Ben said, pausing the camera.

'Oh, you going to invite him out for a pint?' Marty said.

'Nobody likes him,' Ben said. 'I just thought he'd enjoy coming out on one of our trips.'

'These videos make us money, dimwit,' Cara said to her brother. 'The last thing we need is to be babysitting.'

'What's got you in a strop today?' Marty said.

They walked through a blue doorway as Cara ignored him. They still couldn't see Josh but they could hear him banging about ahead.

'How long is this going to take?' Cara said, hunching her shoulders up and making *I'm cold* noises.

'Not long. I told you I want to do a different one from all the others. Start from inside, scout around then head out so we end up with the outside at the end of the shoot.'

He started filming again.

More banging and then they heard shouts.

'He's probably found a teddy bear or something,' Marty said.

Then they heard footsteps running towards them.

'Look what I have!' Josh shouted, his face beaming a smile.

'What's that?' Cara asked, screwing her face up.

Josh was holding up a necklace. 'It was in there!' He pointed to the shower room behind him.

Ben went round him and into the room. Then they heard him throwing his guts up.

'What's in there?' Marty asked.

'A dead woman,' Josh replied.

THREE

'How's the nanny working out?' DS Andy Watt said to Miller as they drove into the entrance of the old nuclear bunker in the disused Barnton quarry off Clermiston Road.

'She's doing well,' Miller said. 'Kim was nervous about starting back to work, but we soon learned to trust the nanny.'

'For God's sake, are we here already?' DCI Paddy Gibb said from the back seat. 'I've only just lit up.'

Miller parked behind a police van. There were a multitude of emergency vehicles parked in the car park of what was once known as a secret bunker, heralding back to the cold war.

'What the hell is this place?' Gibb said as they got out of the car into the cold wind. The sun was out but offered no heat.

'You're old enough to remember this place, Paddy,' Watt said.

'Cheeky bastard.'

'I meant, you being a learned man and all.'

'Don't talk pish.'

'It was part of the RAF Command at Turnhouse during the war,' Miller said, 'until 1952 when it was made into a nuclear bunker. Up to four hundred politicians, civil servants, and military leaders would be housed here for up to thirty days in the case of a nuclear attack.'

'See? How does Miller know this stuff but you're just a bloody ignoramus?' Gibb said as they made their way across to the entrance.

'He read it on his phone.'

'Did you, Miller?' Gibb said.

'Of course not. I know stuff.'

'Well, if you expect me to start reading, forget about it.' Gibb shrugged his overcoat higher.

'Lying sod,' Watt said to Miller behind Gibb's back. 'I saw you.'

'What can I say, Andy?'

They saw figures standing around outside. Paramedics talking, Weaver and Sticks, two of the mortuary assistants, were close by. Sticks, a young Polish woman, smiled at the detectives as they approached.

'Doctor Dagger says to tell you, he's glad for you to be showing up,' she said with a smile.

'You've been in Scotland long enough to know that's an insult,' Gibb said. 'Cheeky wee bugger.'

Sticks giggled.

'And you better not be teaching her stuff like that, Weaver.'

Weaver held his hands out. 'I wouldn't dare, Chief Inspector.'

'Point us in the right direction, if you don't mind,' Miller said.

'Through the door and carry on. The levels are up and down and all over the place but there are uniforms there to make sure nobody gets lost.'

They went in, each man taking out a flashlight, but there were small arc lights at intervals.

'It was set on fire years ago, but somebody bought it and they're turning it into a museum,' Miller said.

'Where did you read that? On the back of your Frosties box this morning?' Watt said.

They were directed through the damp air to the shower room. Kate Murphy and the other pathologist, Jake Dagger, were dressed in their white suits, moving around the body that was lying half in and half out of one of the shower stalls.

'Jesus,' Gibb said.

'Nope, just plain old Jake,' Dagger said, standing up.

'Poor girl,' Kate said. 'What a place to end up.'

'What do we have here?' Gibb said.

Kate stepped closer to him. 'Definitely female. There's a wallet in her pocket and some jewellery. It's hard to put an exact time on this, but it looks like she's been dead for months and was probably murdered elsewhere.'

The smell was awful and Miller had forgotten his little tub of chest rub to put under his nose.

'Any ID?' he asked.

'Adele Mason,' DI Maggie Parks said, standing behind them. She was holding a polythene evidence bag. They turned to look at her. She was dressed in a white suit like the pathologists. 'From looking at her driving license, she was twenty-three.'

'Get her name through the database, Andy' Gibb said. 'See if she's a missing person.'

Watt turned and left the bunker to make the necessary phone call.

'What sort of jewellery did she have?' Miller said, thinking that Adele's death hadn't involved robbery.

'We have it bagged,' she replied, 'but it was a necklace, some rings, a lady's watch and a couple of brooches.'

'High end?'

'The watch is an Omega. Worth a few grand brand new.'

'Have the robbery squad go through it when we get back. Just in case,' Gibb said.

'Who found the body?' Miller said, feeling himself start to shiver in the subterranean bunker.

'A small group of people who were in here filming for their YouTube channel. They're outside being questioned,' Maggie replied.

Miller took one last look at the remains of the young woman, at the dirty anorak that had once been a clean olive colour, the filthy jeans, and tattered trainers. The remnants of her hair that may or may not have been blonde at one time. The rest of her had been claimed by the ravages of decay.

'Let's get out of the way so they can move her to the Cowgate,' Gibb said. The Cowgate was where the City of Edinburgh mortuary was housed.

Back out in the cold, fresh air, they saw a small group of people huddled round in a circle, talking to three of the female detectives on Miller's team; Julie Stott, Steffi Walker, and Hazel Carter. Andy Watt was still on the phone, a little distance away from the group.

'Who are you?' one of them said, walking quickly towards Miller. He looked the man in the eyes and his instinct was to prepare himself for attack, but then he saw the grin appear and realised that the man was different.

'Josh, come here, pal,' one of the other young men said. There were three men and one young woman in total.

Hazel walked over to Miller. 'These are the people who found the body,' she said.

'I found the girl!' Josh said his smile dropping.

'Shut up,' the woman said.

'That's Cara Robertson and her brother, Ben. They film abandoned places for YouTube and they found her.'

She introduced the other two. 'Apparently, Josh is the one who stumbled over her, literally. Then he took a necklace from her.'

'I got it!' he said.

'He just gets excited,' Ben Robertson said to Miller after he'd identified himself.

'What made you go in there?' Miller said. 'It's such a big place.'

'It's like all abandoned places; we're not the first to film it. So everybody tries to film it from a different perspective. We'd just walked through for our first part, starting from inside. We would film the outside too, but we were going to begin inside. Josh was running ahead and he found her.'

'He came out waving the necklace about like it was

a fucking trophy,' Cara said. 'I'm surprised he wasn't wearing her panties.'

'Enough, Cara, for God's sake,' Marty said. Then he turned to look at Miller. 'Josh is special needs.'

'He needs locking up,' Cara said, her voice lower.

'Get a grip,' her brother said.

'He's a fucking perv.'

'Jesus.' Ben shook his head. 'He's like a young boy.'

Cara looked at Miller. 'He's creepy.' She wrapped her arms around herself.

'Was she murdered?' Ben asked.

'Her cause of death hasn't been determined yet,' Miller said. He indicated for Julie Stott to walk away with him and when he was sure he was out of earshot and facing away from the group, he spoke to her. 'Do a background on them all. Especially that girl.'

'Will do, sir,' Hazel said.

'Meantime, have them transported to the station. Preferably not in one group. I want them to give a statement, but keep them separate at the station until they've been questioned again.'

'I'll have that arranged.'

'I'm going to do a search for the victim's next of kin. I'll take Andy with me.'

'Very well.'

Miller turned to look at the small group as Julie walked back over to them. As uniforms escorted them to different vehicles, the woman called Cara turned back to look at him.

There was something in her eyes. Something he'd seen many times before.

Fear.

FOUR

It was starting to rain. Robert Molloy's Range Rover sat on the driveway near the newer part of the cemetery. His driver had stayed in the car, Molloy telling him that he wanted to be alone with his... what? Girlfriend? Companion? Wife? Even though they weren't married.

Whatever, he was standing next to her, holding the umbrella over her. Wind shook the trees, wanting to play with the rain.

Jean Melrose looked at Molloy, tears running down her face, before she stepped forward and placed the bouquet of flowers on her daughter, Abi's, grave.

'Twenty-seven years ago today I gave birth to my little girl,' she said as she stood up straight. Molloy stepped forward a bit and made sure the umbrella covered her again.

'I remember,' he said. 'I was there.'

Her face looked like it was trying to smile, but the tears won. She buried her face into his suit jacket for a moment. 'If it wasn't for you being there, I would have given birth alone.'

'Your husband wasn't the most reliable man on earth.' Molloy looked down at the flowers, already being battered by the rain. 'Has your son been in contact again? Expressing a desire to come here, or for anything else?'

'No. Adam's still angry about his father's death, and since he was technically my stepson, I feel that I shouldn't poke the bear, as it were.'

'You brought him up, Jean. He was, for all intents and purposes, your son.'

'The last time we spoke, he shouted at me on the phone, reminding me that I wasn't flesh and blood.'

'But still. You don't have to give birth to a child to be like a mother.'

'I know. I raised him from when he was a wee boy. But I won't get to see my grandchildren, and it leaves me feeling sad inside like you wouldn't believe.'

Now Molloy was starting to feel angrier. Ever since he and Jean had got together after she had split up from Andy Watt, his feelings for her had intensified. They had been friends for many years, but never in an intimate way. That had changed after they had dinner one night and Molloy had felt something for her like he hadn't felt for a woman since his wife had died years ago.

'Let's go home,' he said, and she looked into his eyes as the rain intensified against the umbrella.

She nodded and they turned away from Abi's gravestone. Jean had moved into his house on Heriot Row. He'd also owned the large house she had lived in up at Colinton which Jean had occupied in exchange for doing some work for him.

After Abi had died in the house, she didn't want to live there anymore, so he had put her up in one of his rental properties – until he asked her to move in a couple of months later. They were happy, except he knew Jean missed her grandchildren just as much as she missed her dead daughter.

The rain tattooed off the umbrella as Molloy opened the back door of the car for Jean. He closed it before going around to the other side and climbing in beside her.

'Home,' he said to the driver, but his thoughts were far from home.

FIVE

'Adele Mason?' Jeni Bridge said. 'The daughter of Clyde Mason?'

'The very one,' Percy Purcell said. 'I wanted to run it by you before we go out and talk to the family.'

'This is not good news, Percy. That man walks about like he has a poker up his arse. I've never met such a condescending prick in my life.'

'I've had many a run-in with him. I couldn't agree more.'

'Still, this has to be done.' She swivelled her chair to look down into the High Street, her thoughts on her own daughter, Lynn, and the problems they'd had. After the debacle in the summer, Lynn had left to go and live with her father through in Glasgow, at least while she went back to college, then she would think about coming back to Edinburgh for the Christmas holidays. Jeni knew Lynn wouldn't be back, not after the attack she'd been through. She would feel safe though there, what with her father being the chief constable.

She turned back to face Purcell. 'Mason thinks he's above the law, so he might give you a hard time. Refer him to me if he has a problem.'

'I will. But he's had his fair share of failures over the years.'

'His ego is so big, he thinks he walks on water,' Jeni said. 'So, go and see him now, then if he gives you hassle, I'll call him and give it to him sideways.'

Purcell stood up. 'It's certainly a strange one. She isn't listed as a missing person so it will be interesting to see what Mason has to say for himself.'

Downstairs in the incident room, he waved Miller over. 'I want you to go with Paddy Gibb to speak to Mason now.'

'What did Jeni say?'

'Shoot from the hip and take no prisoners.'

'Mason is a larger than life character. Did you see him on the *Lorraine Kelly* show?'

'Suzy told me about it. Butter wouldn't melt in his mouth.'

'Must be nice to have his kind of entrepreneurial skills though,' Miller said. 'Everything he touches turns to gold.'

'We should think ourselves lucky he doesn't turn to dealing heroin.'

Gibb and Andy Watt joined Miller. They reached the back door and were hit by a gust of wind passing through the car park.

Miller got in the driver's seat. 'Anything from the robbery boys, Andy?'

'Nothing yet.'

Gibb closed his eyes as Miller shot up towards the tunnel that led to the High Street. 'Here we go. It's Hawick all over again. It's like you have a fucking blackout every time you get behind the wheel, Miller.' Gibb was in the back, fiddling with his cigarettes.

'I wonder how Mason is going to take it when he finds out about his daughter,' Miller said looking at Andy.

'Everybody's different, but if she wasn't listed as missing and she's been dead for months, then it's safe to say he wasn't active in her life for a while.'

'That's true,' Miller said. 'I can't imagine being out of my daughter's life.'

'You've got a way to go, Frank. One is what, eight now? The other is seven months. Long way to go.'

Gibb sat with one hand on the *Oh shit!* handle, the other holding his seatbelt while a cigarette bobbed up and down in his mouth. He looked out of the window as if all this talk about children was getting to him.

Miller headed down Leith Walk and drove along to the Ocean Terminal shopping centre. Opposite was a new office block. He parked in the car park behind.

'Leith is becoming more gentrified every year,' Watt said. 'Remember when we worked down Leith and this place was full of jakies?'

'The jakies have moved on now, but I don't think we're supposed to call them that anymore.'

A wind shot in off the Forth. 'Christ, they wouldn't want to live down here nowadays.' Watt looked at the tall, skinny building with a weak sun bouncing off the blue glass windows. 'They should have called this *Jakey House*, paying homage to the people who paved the way.'

'It's called *Ocean Point*,' Miller informed him as they went into the manned reception area.

'Did you just look that up on your phone as well?'

'I wish Police Scotland had snagged a floor in here for us. We could have sat and gazed out to sea,' Miller said.

'They have bigger windows down here for you, since you're a window licker,' Gibb said to Watt as he felt the warmth of the building envelop them.

A security guard was sitting behind the desk. He directed them to the eighth floor where they entered through glass doors into Mason Enterprises.

'We need to speak to Clyde Mason,' Gibb said. Now he was starting to feel hot.

'Who shall I say is calling?' the girl said.

'DCI Gibb.'

The overly-bright smile of the girl slipped slightly but she remained professional. 'Somebody will take you through.' She looked relieved the task wasn't her responsibility.

The three detectives were shown into a back office down a short corridor after walking past an open-plan area. Clyde Mason was standing looking out through his window.

Miller saw Fife in the distance beyond the Forth.

'What a magnificent sight, don't you think?' Clyde Mason said before he turned to face his guests. None of the detectives answered him. 'Sit, sit,' he said and they each found a chair in the large office.

Clyde Mason was a big man with a large protruding belly. His face was ruddy as if he'd run up the stairs to beat them here. His hair was thinning on top and as his jacket wouldn't button up at the front, he didn't bother trying.

'We're here about your daughter, Adele,' Gibb informed him.

Mason closed his eyes for a second and steepled his fingers across his belly. He looked at them. 'God Almighty, what has she done now?'

'There was a deceased person discovered, who had your daughter's driving license on her. We think it might be her, but we're going to need DNA and dental records.'

Mason swivelled his chair to look out the window again. 'I couldn't believe it when they built this office block. Right in the heart of Leith. I was born and brought up in Leith. When it was the real Leith.' He swivelled back to face them and, for a moment, Miller thought the older man hadn't heard Gibb.

'Do you know where we can get her dental records?' he said to Mason.

'Of course I know where to get them. Can't a man let some news sink in?' His face was going redder now. 'How did she die?'

'We're not sure, yet,' Gibb said. 'That has still to be determined by the pathologists.'

'But she's so decomposed that you need dental records to identify her. Christ. Where was she found?'

'In the old nuclear bunker under Corstorphine Hill,' Watt said.

'What the bloody hell was she doing in there?'

'That's what we were hoping to find out,' Gibb said. 'When was the last time you saw her?'

Mason put his hands on the arms of his chair. 'We haven't spoken in six months or more. I can't be sure.

Time flies, days become weeks, weeks become months. I don't even know when it was.'

'Do you know anybody who would want to hurt her?' Miller asked.

'I always told her, if somebody ever wants to hurt you, tell them Clyde Mason is your father. If that does nothing, I'll send an associate round to have a talk with them. They'll never forget my name after that.'

'Did she hang out with people who might have wanted to harm her?'

'Yes. That's why we fought the last time I saw her. She had a friend. Some rum bastard.'

'What's his name?' Watt said.

'I don't know. I never met him. But that will change if I find out he hurt my daughter, I can assure you.'

'Where was your daughter living?' Gibb said.

'With some hooligans up in Marchmont Crescent.'

'What did she do for a living?'

'Nothing much. That was a bone of contention between us. I offered her a job with my company but she just called me a capitalist bastard and said I could shove my money up my hole. Her words, not mine. So she just lived with some student friends of hers.'

Watt wrote down the address he gave them.

'I don't know if she still lived there the last time she came crawling round, asking for a loan. She could blow hot and cold. I told her she could come back and get it out of there.' He pointed in the general direction of his backside. 'She was definitely living there at some point. I visited her in the flat.'

'Did she wear an expensive watch?' Miller asked, eying up Mason's Rolex.

'I doubt it. I hate to use the term, but my daughter was a tree-hugger. A socialist. She wanted people like me to work our arse off and hand our money over to the lazy bastards who don't want to get out of their pit in the morning. That was another thing we argued about. She told me that my watch would feed a family of ten for a year. I told her to tell somebody who cares. I didn't get up at five o'clock every morning to feed my family just so some sponging shitehouse can play video games into the wee hours.'

'Did she have a best friend?' Gibb asked.

'Some hippie bastard with a name that sounds like a tropical disease. Some ponce whose father was a QC or something. You know what I think QC stands for, don't you? Queer c—'

There was a knock on the door and a secretary poked her head in. 'Your wife is on line two. She's very insistent. Said she'll come round here and rip your... well, she's very upset.' She ducked her head back out like she'd only popped in to throw the hand grenade before beating a hasty retreat.

Miller looked over at Watt, giving him a slight nod.

'Is there a toilet I could use?' Watt said, standing up. Mason pointed at the door in a vague direction. Watt left the room and looked through a glass wall into the office next to Mason's. He knocked and entered. This woman's view was equally impressive, but Watt wasn't in there to look out to sea.

'Sorry to disturb you, but could I speak with you for a minute?'

'Of course. What can I do for you?'

He closed the door behind him.

'I just wanted to ask you a few questions about Mr Mason's daughter.'

'Which one?'

'Adele.'

'She's not in trouble, is she? Although knowing her, it wouldn't surprise me.'

'I'm not at liberty to say, but we're doing some background checks.'

'No, you're not.' The woman sat up straighter in her chair. 'My husband was a copper before he passed. Three detectives don't come calling just for a background check.'

'You're right, Mrs...?'

'Stevenson.'

'Mrs Stevenson, since your husband was one of us, you'll appreciate how we need to keep things confidential. I can't go into details, but if you know anything that might be of help to us, I'd appreciate a few moments of your time.'

'Adele is a little madam, who would have benefited from going over her father's knee for a bloody good skelping when she was younger. Spare the rod and all that. What a lippy little cow she was. Before we moved to these offices, we were in a place along Constitution Street, but they lived in Trinity.'

'Mr Mason did tell us he was born and brought up in Leith.'

'Don't let that flannel fool you. *He* might have been, but his girls were taken home to his big house in Trinity. They went to the best of schools and he showered then with everything they ever wanted. But you know how it is with some spoilt kids; the more you give them, the more they tell you to eff off. That was Adele. What an ungrateful little bitch she was.'

'What's his other daughter's name?'

'Ashley. She wasn't much better but at least she got married and had kids. Adele was much more of a madam though. Came into our offices and looked down her nose at us though she hasn't been in this new office as far as I know.'

'When was the last time you saw Adele?'

The woman stared into space for a moment. 'It must have been more than a year if I remember correctly. Something like that. That was in the other offices. We've only been here a couple of months.'

'How did she seem?' Watt said, starting to feel like he really did need to go use the bathroom.

'Agitated. I was surprised how much she had changed. Almost like she was a homeless person. That's how she was dressed; scruffy. Dirty. I would have given her a pound for a cup of tea if I hadn't known better.'

'Do you know if she was living at home at that time?'

The woman shook her head. 'I heard Mr Mason and his wife arguing one day. The wife wanted Adele to come back home but Mason said not before she had cleaned up her act.'

'Do you think she was on drugs?'

'It certainly looked that way. I can't be sure, of course, but she didn't look like somebody who came from money.'

'Do you think she would buy herself an expensive watch?' Watt said.

'Adele? No way. She was dead against capitalism. Some people would kill just to have a hot meal, yet here was this spoilt wee besom mocking people who have worked hard in life to get where they are. Again, she needed a bloody good skelping, if you ask me. She would have vomited at the thought of wearing an expensive watch.'

'I don't suppose you would know the names of the people she hung out with?'

'No, not their names, but there was one young man she said was her boyfriend; *Lord Snooty* she said his name was. She shortened it to S*nooty* when she was shouting at her father.'

'Do you know where we can get a hold of him?'

'They all lived in the student flat in Marchmont Crescent, last I heard. Maybe he lives there.'

'Thank you. You've been a great help.' He made to leave her office. 'Just one last thing; where's the toilet?'

SIX

What was left of Adele Mason lay on the stainless-steel table, her clothes removed and sent to forensics. What had once been a beautiful young woman was now a torn and reeking mess, roughly resembling the shape of a human being.

'How did Mason take it when you told him about his daughter?' Percy Purcell said as Miller came into the post mortem room.

'He was shocked but his daughter had been in decline for a long time.' He acknowledged the presence of Kate Murphy, Julie Stott, and Julie Walker.

'Terrible business,' Dr Leo Chester said, coming into the room. 'It's always a tragedy when a death involves somebody young.'

They were suited up and the detectives stood back a little from the table. Each of them had the chest rub under their nose, breathing in menthol rather than death and decay.

'Obvious signs of death, doctor?' Purcell said.

'I examined her a little while ago, and we noticed the large cut across her neck. Rather hard to miss. She'd had her throat cut and Kate here saw a knife mark where it had hit a rib. We're thinking that she was stabbed and had her throat cut. We'll look into it further of course, and you're all welcome to watch, but this is definitely a murder, no doubt about it.'

Purcell turned to Miller. 'I read the preliminary from Maggie Parks and her forensics crew. They said that they reckon she was still alive when they went into the bunker. There wasn't a lot of blood, but there was some spatter found on the walls near where she was found. From the injuries the doc described, it could be she had already been stabbed and then taken there where she had her throat cut. That would explain the spatter but no pool of blood.'

'DCI Gibb went to the address we were given, but nobody was home, so we're going back,' Miller said.

'Find anybody who knew her. Get them interviewed. Have you spoken to her mother yet?'

'Not yet. I came here first while DCI Gibb went to Marchmont.'

'Go and speak to her now. I'll call Gibb and tell him to go with you.'

'Yes, sir.'

Miller left the stench of the mortuary and got back to his car in the car park.

Paddy Gibb pulled into the rear car park of the station. Jeni Bridge was outside smoking, chatting with Miller.

'Appreciate them while they're young, Frank. You never know how they're going to turn out.' She blew smoke into the cold air where it drifted away.

'Just a couple of years ago, I didn't have a girlfriend, and now I'm married with a stepdaughter and a daughter. My life already feels like it's on the fast-track.'

'The older you get, the faster each year passes. My old man used to tell me that, and I didn't believe him. Now I wish I could turn the clock back. Enjoy my little girl more.'

'I'm taking on board everything you say, commander. Trust me on that one.'

'Everybody has regrets. My problem was holding on too tight. I should have given Lynn a little bit more leeway.'

'From what I saw, you did nothing wrong. Kids will attach themselves to others, whether we allow them to or not.'

'You're wise beyond your years. But I know what

you mean; Lynn met that prick Mark and he dragged her down. Who knew that Andy Watt's girlfriend would have a daughter who was into drugs.'

'Her deceased father was at fault there,' Miller said.

'Lynn's living through in Glasgow with her father again, now that she's back at uni. He'll keep an eye on her, but he also has another child with his younger wife.' She took a drag on the cigarette. 'His *much* younger wife. Just wait 'til she wants it twice in one night, let's see if his ticker won't give out then.'

Paddy Gibb got out of the car from the driver's seat and opened a back door. He took out his pack of cigarettes before spotting Jeni Bridge. He had a look of *Oh shit* on his face.

'If you'll excuse me,' Miller said.

'Just remember what I told you, Frank. It will save you a lot of heartache in the future.'

'I will.'

'Try not to burn the upholstery, DCI Gibb,' Jeni shouted over.

'I'm just holding them. I'm trying to quit and I feel this helps,' he replied.

'Whatever keeps you off the ledge. Just remember to crack a window.'

He pretended not to hear her and got in the back, closing the door.

'You want me to drive?' Miller said, opening the driver's door and poking his head in. Watt was over in the front passenger seat.

'That's like asking if you want to swap deckchairs on the Titanic. Get in and shut the door for fuck's sake.'

The car was still running. Miller got in and turned the car around and headed back up to the High Street through the tunnel.

'You're fifty-one next week you told me,' he said to Watt.

'I did. And I don't want you going to great expense for my present. But don't tell me; I want it to be a surprise.'

'I'm getting you fuck all. How's that for a surprise?' Gibb said.

'That comes as no surprise to me,' Miller said.

'But you boys are going to take me to the pub and I won't be putting my hand in my pocket, right?' Watt said as Gibb lit a cigarette in the back.

'You already mentioned that. It wouldn't be any different from any other night,' Gibb said, blowing smoke into the front.

'Jeni said to crack the window, selfish sod,' Watt said, opening the passenger window.

'She just has to say that in case this comes back to bite her in the arse.'

'Second-hand smoke kills,' Miller said.

'So does driving like an old fanny going to church on Sunday, so get the fucking boot down.'

'Make up your mind; one minute I drive like a maniac and the next like a wee school lassie.'

'Rule of thumb from now on; if I'm about to smoke in the car and Jeni Bridge is watching, drive it like you stole it.'

Miller drove down Broughton Street as Gibb continued to poison them with his toxic fumes.

SEVEN

It didn't take long to get to their destination, a detached pile in Lomond Road in the heart of Trinity, opposite Trinity Bowling Club. There was a small driveway at the front, leading to what might have been an attached garage many moons ago, but somebody somewhere along the line had converted it into another room.

'Like this house needs another room,' Watt said, looking at the property.

The woman who answered the door looked like she was either Clyde Mason's trophy wife or a neighbour. Turned out she was neither.

'I'm Ashley Melrose,' she said. She looked past Gibb and Miller at Watt. There was a look that passed between them, as if they knew each other.

'We're here to speak to Mrs Mason,' Gibb said, taking the lead.

'Of course. Please, come through. My mother has a friend round as well. She's very upset.'

The three detectives walked along to the living room, following Ashley. She showed them into a large room, expensively furnished. A woman sat on a couch, crying into a hanky, another older woman sitting beside her with a comforting arm around her shoulders.

'Mother,' Ashley snapped. 'You have visitors.' There was no compassion in her voice. Maybe a hint of embarrassment, but no empathy.

The older women both looked up at the same time, the neighbour dropping her arm down as if she'd been caught doing something she shouldn't.

'We're police officers,' Miller said, in case she thought they were Jehovah's Witnesses who had actually made it into the house. 'We've come to talk to you about Adele.'

The neighbour stood up. 'I can come back later, Frances.'

Frances Mason nodded her head and kept her gaze on the departing neighbour, almost begging her not to go, but the three detectives in the room dictated her exit.

'Could you make some more tea, Ashley?' Frances said.

'Of course.' Ashley left the room and Frances gazed at the men as if she was waiting for the punchline, that they were really here to tie her up and rob her.

Miller and Gibb seated themselves.

'If you'll excuse me a moment,' Andy Watt said and followed Ashley out of the room. He found her in the kitchen.

'You looked surprised to see me,' she said, filling the kettle from the tap. She kept her back to Watt as the kettle filled.

'Of course I'm surprised to see you. You're Jean Melrose's daughter-in-law but apart from that, I don't know much about you, Ashley.'

She turned to face him and smiled. 'Well, now you know that my father is Clyde Mason, my mother's first name is Frances and my sister Adele is dead.'

She put the kettle on its base and pressed a button.

'You don't seem very cut up about it.' Watt nodded as Ashley held up a mug. 'Coffee for me, please.'

'I liked you a lot, Andy. I really did.'

'I know. You told me often enough when you were pished in the pub and wanted me to hail you a taxi.'

She giggled like a schoolgirl. 'Those were good times. You have the sense of humour I would have liked my husband to have, but he's like a plank in company. Invariably, the conversation turns to his work. I don't know about you, but I got bored hearing about his criminal cases.'

'The man's an advocate. I thought that was a prerequisite to join the faculty.'

'See? I miss those times. Did you know I was in Logie Baird's one night and I was about to come across but I thought you wouldn't want a drink with me.'

'I'm a detective, of course I knew you were there. I didn't want to back you into a corner. I figured that you would have come across and spoken to me if you felt comfortable.'

'I'd still like to, Andy. If I'm in there and I see you.'

'Feel free. You were almost my daughter-in-law. You're like family to me, Ashley.'

'I'll join you the next time, I promise. But to be fair, you were with another woman.'

'That's Kate, my girlfriend,' Watt said.

'I'm glad you moved on. To be honest, I'm glad you and Jean aren't together anymore. You know she's a friend of Robert Molloy's, don't you?'

'I did find that out.'

'Now she's his girlfriend,' Ashley said, popping teabags into mugs. 'Did you know that?'

'No, I didn't know Jean was Molloy's girlfriend now.' He stared off into space for a moment.

'Don't worry, I had a drink with her one day, and I came right out and asked her bluntly if she had ever passed on any information that she had got from you. She said, Molloy had asked her to, a long time ago, but she had flatly refused. He was throwing business her way but that was crossing the line she said.'

'And you believed her?'

'I did. I'm a solicitor, too, remember? Like my husband was, before he became a devil.'

Watt's eyebrows rose.

'Devils are trainee advocates,' she explained.

'Makes sense.'

The kettle switched itself off and she poured while Watt took milk from the fridge. He added a splash to the mugs.

'You don't seem too upset about your sister,' he said, putting the milk away.

Ashley smiled. 'What's to be upset about? She was an obnoxious human being. Approaching thirty, no husband, no career, absolutely hated my father for making money, yet she asked him on many occasions for *a loan*,' she said, using air quotes. 'She asked me for the same thing but I told her I wouldn't throw a couple of pounds into a hat for her if I saw her sitting on the pavement. She told me I should go forth and multiply.'

'When was the last time you saw her?'

Ashley stirred the cups of tea and put them on a little tray, adding a bowl of sugar. Watt picked up his own cup of coffee.

'Hold that thought, Andy.' She carried the tray through to the living room and came back.

'The last time I saw Adele was around six months ago, maybe longer, I can't quite remember. It was so erratic. That last time was when she told me I was a bad sister. Like she was Cinderella. But my dad worked hard for all of this. Have you met him?'

'We spoke to him earlier at his office. He did say he was brought up in Leith.'

'Trinity is a sort of extension of Leith, with a little stretch of the imagination. But yes, he was, and he made some decent money. I mean, he wouldn't have moved to Barnton, but he saw this as sticking close to his roots. Adele and I had the best opportunities. She chose to go down a different path from me. I wanted to work hard and make some decent money. She just wanted to bum around. She dropped out of university when she fell in with the wrong crowd. She was a real arsehole.'

'Not wanting to speak ill of the dead,' Watt said.

'I know that sounds rough, Andy, but we drifted apart. We had nothing in common if you discount our parents, and we didn't have the same interests. I have two kids, she has two boyfriends. I drive a Mercedes, she drives people away. I spend money on expensive clothes, she gets hers from charity shops.'

She drank from her own mug, holding it in two hands, and looked away for a second, as her mind wandered somewhere else.

'You didn't ask anything about her death,' Watt said.

'I didn't need to. My father called me after my mother went all hysterical and called him, fuelled by a mixture of anger and sorrow. He called me to let me know and I came down here.' She drank more tea. The kitchen was warm and comfortable, and it might have been a pleasant visit if it weren't for the fact that there had been a death in the family.

'Did he tell you where she was found?'

Ashley nodded. 'In the old bunker at Corstorphine Hill.'

'Any idea why somebody would take her there?'

'None at all. I knew it existed, but I didn't know anything about it until I Googled it earlier. But it seems that volunteers are turning it into a museum. You should check them out.'

'Thank you, Sherlock. We already have their names and some of the team are talking to them.'

'It's the solicitor in me, Andy.'

'Are you still with the same firm?'

She shook her head and drank more tea. 'No. I jumped ship. I'm with a smaller firm now. Richard Sullivan's office.'

'Richard Sullivan? Robert Molloy's arch enemy?'

'Oh, he's hardly that. Don't make him sound like

Superman's Kryptonite. They just didn't see eye-to-eye for a while.'

'That's an understatement. Robert Molloy found out that Frank Miller's first wife was his daughter and Sullivan had arranged the adoption. He then thought Sullivan was behind Carol's death.'

'I heard the story.'

'People think the man's a shark.'

'He knows how to make money, that's for sure. He's built up a small team, people who trust him.'

Watt drank some of the coffee, which was good. 'Are the offices still down at the Shore?'

'Yes, we're still there.'

'What does Adam think of that?'

Ashley shrugged. 'I don't give a crap. Adam and I have split up.'

'Jesus, I'm sorry to hear that. When did this happen?'

'A month ago.'

'Obviously, I didn't hear about it since I'm no longer in the loop,' Watt said.

'It's no big deal. Adam changed when he became an advocate. He just promoted himself to God status.'

'How are the kids?'

'They'll get through it. He still sees them.'

'I'm sure Sullivan will keep you right,' Watt said.

'My dad will keep me right. He and Adam got on well enough when I was still married, but now he's not quite so happy with him.'

'I don't blame him.' Watt looked at her. 'Do you mind me asking what went wrong?'

Ashley took a deep breath before answering. 'He was cheating on me. I don't know who with, but his whole routine changed. When I confronted him with it, he confessed that he was. He didn't even have the decency to pull a beamer, Andy.'

'Bastard.' But Watt could feel his own face going red. He'd cheated on Ashley's mother-in-law after all. 'How long was it going on before you found out?'

He wouldn't say but it was a while. I'd noticed a change in his behaviour months before I confronted him.'

'I'm sorry to hear that, love. But if I'm being honest, Adam and I didn't see eye-to-eye. He hated me dating his mother.'

'I know. There's no love lost there. He nearly pissed his pants when you said you were moving in with his mother. He advised her against it.'

'I thought as much. I couldn't see him throwing me a party.' Watt put his mug down. 'In your father's office, I spoke with Mrs Stevenson. She told me Adele had a boyfriend she called *Lord Snooty*. Did you ever meet him?'

'I never heard her talk about him. But she had a few boyfriends. All student types. I think she was attracted by them being the lazy bastard type.'

'We went to the flat in Marchmont but nobody was in.'

'Her friends would be in class. When they were out, she would just ponce about all day.'

'How did she get money?' Watt said.

'She was left a trust fund by my grandmother. We both were. I invested mine, Adele lives off hers. Lived. It wasn't a fortune but it was enough to keep her off the streets.'

'That doesn't sound like somebody who was a diehard liberal socialist.'

'They hate capitalism until they need money for their next fix.'

'Was Adele on drugs?' Watt grabbed his mug. It made him think of Jean's own daughter and the scumbag father she had. And by default, Adam's father too.

'It was hard to tell at times. I don't think she was a hardened junkie, though I think she dabbled when she was bored. But I assume that she would have been hooked by now had she tried the hard stuff.'

'The boss wanted her name run past the drug boys and the robbery boys.'

'And girls, Andy. This is the age of equality.'

'It was just a phrase. Some of those lassies on the drugs team would rip us boys a new one. I tip my hat to them, believe me.' There was silence between them for a few moments. 'I miss the girls.'

'They miss you too, Andy.'

'I know things had started to go downhill between me and Jean before I slept with that other woman, but sometimes I wish I hadn't been a stupid old twat.' Watt shook his head.

'We can't turn the clock back. But I *can* ask the girls if they would like to go to the pictures with you and me one day.'

Watt smiled. 'I don't know how Jean would take that.'

'I know she's their grandmother but she's about to be my ex mother-in-law. They're my daughters as well as Adam's, so if Jean doesn't like that, she can bog off.'

'It's a date.'

'Don't say that too loud, or Adam might get the wrong idea.' Ashley smiled at him.

'It's not something he should ever voice to my face. I just want to see the bairns, the wee girls I looked on as my own grandkids.'

She put a hand on his arm. 'They're going to love seeing you again, don't worry.'

They chatted for a few minutes longer until Miller came into the kitchen. 'Ready to go, DS Watt?'

'Yes, sir.' He put his mug down again. 'Give me a call,' he said to Ashley.

She kissed him on the cheek. 'Take care, Andy.'

EIGHT

'Christ, I'm here more than I'm over at the club in George Street,' Michael Molloy said. He took the glass from his father. They were in Robert Molloy's office in the new flashy hotel on the North Bridge.

'It's not like I'm asking you over to the Sally Army hostel.' They clinked glasses. 'Sit. I want to have a word with you.'

Robert sat on a leather couch while Michael sat in a chair.

There was a knock on the door and Greg Sampson, Robert's head of security, opened the door and showed Robert's guests in.

Adrian Jackson walked in, bowler hat on, walking stick in his right hand.

'You never told me Jackson was coming,' Michael said.

'You never asked.'

Michael made a face until he saw Rita Mellon follow Jackson into the room, then his face lit up and he stood to greet them. He ignored Jackson and walked up to Rita.

'Mrs Mellon. I hope life is treating you well,' he said.

'It is indeed, Michael. And how have you been since we last met?'

'You know how it is; working hard to keep the old man afloat. Working long hours for little pay. Like yourself, I imagine.'

'Oh yes. Rock 'n' roll lifestyle.'

Jackson turned to them both. 'Mrs Mellon lives with my nephew in a new apartment where the old Royal Infirmary once sat. Hardly living cheek and jowl with a bunch of schemie junkies.'

'He does look after me, I have to admit,' Rita said in a lower voice. 'Just don't tell him I said so.'

Jackson shook his head as Robert walked over to the drinks cabinet. 'Usual, Adrian?'

'That would be most pleasurable, Robert. My palate hasn't been courted by your twenty-five-year-old malt for a while. It's a bit early for imbibing, but the pull of the current is too strong.'

Robert poured him a glass and an orange juice for Rita.

'Does he always talk like that?' Michael said.

Rita shrugged in a non-committal way.

'Ignorance is the devil's playground,' Jackson said.

'If you ever want to jump ship and come work for me, just give me a shout,' Michael said, passing the glass of orange juice over to her.

'Rita knows what side her bread is buttered on,' Jackson said, sitting down on a couch.

'Look at this; two men fighting over me. I haven't had that since Malkie slashed a wido in a pub one night.'

'Your ex-husband always was a bit uncouth,' Jackson said.

'There's going to be no slashing in here, I can assure you,' Robert said.

Rita sat down next to Jackson, still smiling.

'Now that we're all gathered here, I'll begin,' Robert said.

'You sound just like our old church minister,' Rita said, taking a sip of the orange juice.

Except when he goes to visit a parishioner, it isn't to offer Godly advice, it's to administer a sermon with a claw hammer, Jackson mused, but kept the thought to himself.

'I thought it was a social visit,' he said, 'since our monthly meeting with George Stone and Kerry Hamilton isn't scheduled for another couple of weeks.'

'No, no, this is another matter altogether,' Robert said. 'I need your help, Adrian.'

'Really? Something that the great Robert Molloy can't manage? I must say I'm flattered.'

'Don't be,' Michael said. 'He just wants some arsehole taken care of.'

'Shut up, for God's sake,' said his father, putting his glass down. 'It's not as if I want somebody thrown off the Forth rail bridge. If that was the case, I have plenty of personnel at my disposal.' He looked at Jackson. 'Please excuse my son's outburst. It seems that when a job requires potential violence, he starts foaming at the mouth.'

Jackson waved away the apology. 'I'm sure if it's in my power, the job can be done.'

'It is. And it can. And of course, I would owe you a favour. And that's something you can take to the bank.'

'I must say, this is very exciting,' Rita said.

'No offense, Mrs Mellon, but this won't be a job that you'll be tagging along on,' Michael said.

'I know, but it's nice being in the loop. Brian will be excited as well.'

'Now, that *is* somebody who will be involved,' Robert said. 'If you don't mind, that is,' he said to Jackson.

'Not at all. I don't want the lad going soft.'

'Good. But before I tell you what I need, I feel I need to explain how delicate this situation is.'

'I'm all ears.'

'I'm asking you on board because I can't be directly involved. And when I explain, all will become clear.'

Jackson finished off his whisky and held out his glass. 'Michael, if you would do the honours.'

Michael looked like he wanted to take the glass and ram it in Jackson's face, but his father nodded and he refilled the glass. Then he sat back down and whispered something to Rita. Jackson thought the conversation between them probably involved exchanging bodily fluids, and he made an effort to keep his lunch down.

Then he saluted Robert with his glass.

'Let's get down to business.'

NINE

'You were pretty cosy,' Gibb said, the cigarette bobbing up and down in his mouth as Miller pulled away from the house.

'*And* she kissed him goodbye,' Miller added.

'If you two think you're going to get under my skin, you can bog off, the pair of you,' Watt said.

'A kiss *and* insulting his superior officers. You would have been locked up for that years ago, son. I mean, I can't say I'm not impressed. I know you're a fast worker but—'

'She's Jean's daughter-in-law. She was married to Jean's son, but now they've split up. I was in there getting the skinny on her sister. Adele was the black sheep of the family.'

'Just talking? Now I'm not so impressed,' Gibb said.

'Give it a rest, eh, Paddy?'

'Shoe's on the other foot now. I'm usually the one getting slagged.'

'She's like my daughter. I'm going to meet up with her and her wee girls so we can go to the pictures. Her husband is a wanker, but those wee lassies are like my own grandchildren.'

Gibb reached forward and patted Watt's shoulder. 'Fair enough, son. You'll be glad that tosser is out of the picture then?'

'We never liked each other. He's blown it with Ashley now though. Putting it around, so he was,' Watt said.

'What does he do for a living?' Miller asked.

'He's an advocate. He thinks he has a magic wand that he waves and a woman's knickers will drop.'

'Sounds like a right tool,' Gibb said. 'Talking of which, get us back up to Marchmont. Those rocket scientists should have finished their classes for the day by now. And try not to put the fucking car through a hedge.'

They found a parking space and this time when Gibb rang the buzzer next to the name on the panel, a voice answered. He identified himself and they were buzzed in.

A young woman was waiting for them at the door. 'Look, if it's about all that crap that was left on the pavement last May, I told the old boot in the next stair that it was nothing to do with me. The bloke who moved out dumped it there.'

'It's not,' Gibb said, introducing the two others. 'Can we come in?' He made it sound like he wasn't going to take *no* for an answer.

She stood back and let them walk inside. She was about twenty with dirty blonde hair. 'Nick, it's the cops!' she shouted. They heard sudden movement and Miller and Watt reached for their extendable batons, but the figure ran out of the living room and went into the bathroom, slamming the door behind him.

'Well, that's not suspicious,' Watt said. 'Before he flushes, tell him we're here about Adele Mason. That will save him a trip to the local scumball who he gets his baggies from.'

'How dare you,' the girl said. 'Nick has irritable bowel syndrome.'

'I have irritable *student* syndrome,' Gibb said. 'Get Nick out of the bathroom so we can have a word with the two of you. That way, we won't have to repeat ourselves.'

'I thought you lot liked the sound of your own voices?' she said, squeezing past Watt. She stopped and knocked on the door. 'Come out of there, Nick. They want to talk about that tramp you were shagging.'

'We were just good friends,' Nick said as he poked

his head out of the bathroom. His accent was upper class English and Watt wondered if this was the man Adele had called *Lord Snooty*.

They sat down in the living room on furniture that wouldn't have looked out of place in a charity shop.

'Right, let's get some names before we start,' Watt said.

'Linda,' the young woman said.

'Really? This is the way you want to play it? We can haul you down to the station to help with our enquiries.'

'For what reason?'

'Suspicion of murder, for a start,' Gibb said. 'Yes, that's a real thing, in case you thought that was only on TV.'

'Murder? What are you talking about?'

'Last name?' Watt said.

'Featherstone.'

'And you?' Miller said to the young man.

'Tarquin Tarshall.'

Watt scribbled the name down. 'That's not something you're making up, is it?'

'You haven't heard of him?' Linda said.

'Oh, you mean Tarquin of the world famous Tarshalls?' Gibb said. 'I thought you said his name was Nick?'

'Nick's his middle name, what everybody calls him.

He was voted best new breakout act at last summer's *Perrier* comedy awards.' Linda managed to look both proud of Tarshall and disgusted at Gibb all at the same time.

'I must have missed that show,' Gibb said.

'Probably past your bedtime,' sneered Tarshall.

'What?'

'Nothing.'

'Let me see some form of ID,' Miller said.

Tarshall got up with a face that looked like a blanket a dog had just pissed on. He came back with his wallet and took his license out. Gibb looked at it, then handed it back. Nodded to Watt.

'Now are you going to tell us what this is all about?' asked Linda.

'A body was found this morning and we believe it to be that of Adele Mason,' Miller said.

Linda clamped a hand over her mouth while Tarshall's bottom lip headed south towards the carpet.

Linda removed her hand. 'Adele's dead?'

'We're sure but we're waiting for DNA,' Watt said. 'How well did you know her?'

'She lived here for a while. Always flitting in and out. And *he* thought he would take advantage of her,' she replied, nodding to Tarshall.

'Hey, that's unfair,' Tarshall said. 'I only asked her out for a drink.'

'You were her boyfriend?' Gibb said.

'We were friends but then we started dating. But she was like a wild horse.'

'She was a nag,' Linda said.

Tarshall shot her a look. 'She couldn't be tamed. She was a free spirit.'

Linda cured her lip. 'She was a whore. When she threw Tarshall away like he was a piece of garbage, he went crawling to her and she told him she had met somebody else. Somebody more mature. Somebody who gave her the excitement she craved.'

'Did she call you *Lord Snooty*?' Watt asked.

Tarshall looked at him like he had just stepped from the mothership. 'What? No. Of course she didn't call me that. What, just because I have an English accent you think you can come in here and insult me?' He folded his arms and sat back on the couch.

'You don't have to look like somebody just took your ball,' Gibb said.

'Maybe the older bloke was this *Snooty* guy,' Linda said, her eyes beginning to go red.

'When was the last time you saw her?' Miller said.

'Not since before the summer. She was invited along to Tarquin's big show, but she didn't appear. I tried calling her after that, but I didn't get a reply. I was worried of course, but anybody who knew her would have understood that she couldn't be tied down. She always said she was free as a bird. But we all assumed this older man was the centre of her world now.'

'Did you ever hear from her again?' Watt said.

'No.'

Tarshall shook his head and Gibb stood up, followed by the other two detectives. 'If you can think of anything else that would help us, please give us a call,' he said, handing over a business card.

They left the two students and walked back downstairs to the car.

'Do you believe them?' Watt said.

'I don't think that ponce has it in him,' Gibb said.

'I think they talk the talk,' Miller added. 'I've seen their sort before.'

They left Marchmont just as the rain was starting.

TEN

Adam Melrose sat back in his chair, his hands behind his head. He was finishing up for the day and the pub was calling him.

His assistant, a young woman with a Gaelic name he couldn't spell so he shortened it to Si, was hanging on his every word.

'And when you've typed that report up, we can go and have dinner. I know of a new place that's opened down by the Shore.'

'You never stop trying, do you?' she said, smiling.

'Of course not, Si. How could I disappoint a lady who is so obviously after my charm?' He smiled at her.

'Oh, there's a man here to see you. He said he's friends with Richard Sullivan.'

'Sullivan? He didn't say he was sending somebody

along.' Melrose sat forward, bringing his hands down to his desk. 'What's his name?'

'Brian Jackson.'

Melrose looked at his watch. 'Okay, send him in. I can give him five minutes but no more.'

Si left the office and a minute later, Brian entered without knocking.

'Come in,' Melrose said with a hint of sarcasm in his voice.

Brian sat down before being asked. Already, Melrose didn't like the man and made a mental note to chew Sullivan out for sending this reprobate to him. First though, he'd hear him out.

'What can I do for you?' he asked the young man.

'It's not me you have to do something for,' Brian said, sitting back in the chair.

'I'm sorry, did you get lost somewhere and end up in here by mistake or something?'

'You're Adam Melrose, aren't you?'

'Yes.'

'Nice offices here in Parliament Square.'

'What do you want?' Melrose was starting to lose his patience with this man.

'Has anybody ever told you that you have hands like a girl's?'

Melrose stood up quickly. 'I don't know who the

hell you think you're talking to, but you need to get out of my office right now.'

The door opened again. 'Relax, Adam.' Adrian Jackson walked in and closed the door behind him. He took his bowler hat off and laid it on a side table then sat down beside his nephew, his walking cane resting between his legs. Melrose was still standing staring across at them.

'I already told you to sit, Adam, and I am not a man who lends himself to repetition.'

Melrose sat down. He was used to having lowlifes in his office, but these two brought it to a whole new level.

'I'm listening.'

'We're friends of a friend. Somebody who is close friends with your mother.'

'Is this what it's all about? My fucking mother?' He made a face as if there was a sudden bad smell in the office.

'Please have some respect when it comes to Jean.'

'Did that old bitch send you here?'

Jackson looked at Brian for a second. 'It seems there's an air of confusion.' He looked at Melrose. 'Your mother is upset that you don't see her now. It seems that you blame her for your father's death.'

'Right, I've heard enough. Why don't you both get

the fuck out of my office.' He looked past them to the door. 'Si!'

No reply.

'Si! Show these two reprobates out.'

Nothing.

Now Melrose looked unsure of himself.

'Oh dear, it seems as if your young assistant is otherwise disposed.'

'If you've touched her...'

Jackson laughed. 'Oh, I've touched her alright. But only to shake her hand when I was introduced to her earlier today.'

'What are you talking about?' Melrose stared at Jackson.

'I was suitably informed that Si, as you know her though it's not her real name, came to you with an excellent CV, and that you hired her on the spot. No doubt her ample breasts and shapely legs helped her obtain employment in this fine establishment.'

Melrose's face started to go red. 'What do you mean, not her real name?'

'Not important. What's more important is you trying to sleep with her. Does the owner of this advocacy know you're trying to sleep with your assistant?'

'Get out.'

'Before the finale? Why the rush, old chum? Don't

you want to know how you can stay out of solitary in Saughton?'

'What are you blethering about?'

'Nice laptop you have there.' Jackson nodded to the HP machine that was sitting on the desk.

'It's functional.'

'And it's full of porn. Not the sort you would want shown around the office. I mean, dark web stuff. Really vile, sick, perverted filth.'

'What? I don't think so, pal.' Melrose opened the machine up and looked through it. 'You're full of shit. Now, I don't know what game you're trying to play, but I want you out of here or I'm going to call the police.'

'I'm glad you like the clone. It was swapped out for the real one this morning while you were in court. The one that has all the filth – and your name on it – is in our safekeeping.'

'I don't believe you. This is the machine I always use.'

'Look again,' Brian said. 'Open up the photos, the documents.'

Melrose did and found all of his files were gone.

'You erased them. What the hell is going on?'

'No, we didn't erase them. I told you, we put all the filth on your machine. Or rather, Si did. Over the past month. Filled it up. Images that would make a grown man cry. A normal man, not a pervert like you.'

'I didn't download anything.'

'*We* know that. *You* know that. But the police won't know that. They will take the machine apart, and they'll find all your files. They'll know it's your laptop, and they'll find all the filth. Then you'll be put away for a long time. Si will testify against you. We'll drum up witnesses, phantom people you had drinks with in a bar, who will swear you started talking about being a lowlife scumbag.'

'You're blackmailing me?'

'Adam, I can assure you that is exactly what we're doing. We will fuck you over sideways if you don't meet our demands. Si will swear you had two laptops and you asked her to keep one for you. She didn't know what was on it but you asked her to do some work at home, and she found those images.'

'I don't believe it. I don't believe *you*.'

Jackson took a coin from his pocket and tossed it in the air. Caught it and slapped it onto the back of his left hand. 'Fifty-fifty chance it's heads. That's not bad odds. Those odds are the same that we haven't touched your laptop. We do have it, by the way. But put filth on it? Fifty-fifty chance that we're shitting you and we're bluffing. Fifty-fifty chance we really did and Si will go to the police with it. Do you want to take the chance?'

Melrose sat and looked at Jackson, the wheels in his head turning.

'Okay, Adam, I'm going to give you one chance here; call. Heads or tails.'

Melrose made eye contact with him. Jackson didn't blink but kept the smile on his face.

'Heads.'

Jackson lifted his hand but kept the coin shielded. Then he took it and put it back in his pocket. 'Now you'll be wondering if it was heads or tails, but you'll never know. Are you willing to take the risk with your laptop?'

Jackson and Brian got up to go.

'What do you want?' Melrose said, standing up.

'Your mother is missing her grandchildren. You're getting divorced. She just wants to see the kids on a regular basis. Make it happen.'

Melrose was used to appearing in court on behalf of a client and he knew when he was beaten.

'I'll talk to my ex. Whenever she is agreeable, I'll take the kids to see Jean.'

'Make it soon, Adam. Robert Molloy is not a man to be fucked with.'

Melrose watched as the two men left the office. He looked out of his office window and saw them walking across Parliament Square with his assistant. The woman he had known for a short time, the woman he'd called Si, wouldn't be having dinner with him. Ever again.

Outside, the young woman held onto Brian as he held up an umbrella. Jackson winged it, the rain bouncing off his bowler hat, at least until they got back to the Range Rover they had come in, which had been supplied by Molloy.

'You have the laptop secure?' Jackson asked her.

'Somebody from Robert's employ took it the day I swapped it. But let me ask you; there isn't filth on it, is there?'

'Jesus, no, of course not. Molloy wouldn't go for that. He just wanted me to plant the seeds. It was the lesser of two evils; Adam Melville gets to keep his kneecaps.'

'I thought he was a sleazy prick anyway. I'll be glad to be back working in Robert's hotel.'

'This time tomorrow, you will be.'

They got back in the car and Jackson looked up at Melrose's office window. It was empty.

ELEVEN

'I'm going on the stage,' Lou Purcell said to his father.

'The one going furthest west, I hope.'

'Oh, you'd like that, eh?' They were in Logie Baird's bar.

Frank Miller came over with some glasses, followed by Andy Watt.

'Don't you listen to your son, Lou,' Paddy said. 'He'd be in tears if you left here.'

'Tears laughing, Paddy,' said Percy.

'Oh away, man.'

'But anyway, just to clarify,' Lou added as Miller and Watt sat down, 'I'm doing an amateur play.'

'What brought this on?' asked Gibb, raising his glass to Miller, who had bought the round.

'I'm having fun working with Bruce, but I wanted to get a hobby as well.'

'It's better than sitting about doing nothing,' Miller said.

'That's what I said!' Lou drank some of the whisky that Miller had brought over. 'I've been thinking about becoming a thespian for a while now.'

'Are they the people who come round the doors selling religion?' Percy said.

'Maybe on your planet, son, but where we live, we thespians are stage or screen actors.'

'I know, Dad. How are people going to know I'm insulting you if you keep explaining things?'

'Where are you going to be acting?' Gibb said.

'I'm not sure yet. First of all, I'll be helping a friend of mine.'

'Who do you know that's an actor?' Percy said.

'Somebody I just recently met. In here in fact.'

'Really?' Miller said. 'What's his name?'

Lou grinned as the door opened, and he stood up. 'Not *he*,' he said. 'Same again, lads?'

They agreed on the same again and turned to see a beautiful woman standing looking around. She smiled and waved when she saw Lou. She unfastened her coat and Lou rushed over to take it from her.

'Come on over and I'll introduce you,' Lou said to her, indicating to the barman that another round was required. He also ordered a G&T.

'Sonya, this is my son, Percy, and some of his co-workers.' He introduced them in turn.

'Nice to meet you, gentlemen,' she said.

'If Dad's coerced you in any way to come and meet him here, just let me know and I'll sort him out.'

She laughed. 'Don't worry, I'm here under my own volition.'

'If you'll excuse us, Sonya and I have to go over some lines.' Lou picked up Sonya's drink and took it and his own over to another table as Watt went to the bar to get the other drinks that Lou had paid for.

'I bloody well knew he was up to something,' Percy said. 'A bath, twice in one week, he told me. *And* after-shave. Next thing I know, he'll be telling me he brushed his teeth as well.'

Miller laughed. 'Let him have some fun.' He looked over at the woman; she looked to be around forty. Blonde hair, with a shapely figure; he thought that Percy would do well to date a woman like her, never mind his father.

'Fun? His bloody heart will give out. I hope he knows I signed a DNR form.'

'What a way to go though, eh?' Watt said.

'You should be so lucky,' Gibb said to him.

'I'm going to ignore that remark, Paddy, as I know it comes from a bottomless pit of jealousy and resentment.'

'I'm going to miss you when you move out this weekend.'

'Yeah, okay. Didn't you say, *Don't let the door bang your arse on the way out*?' Watt drank some lager.

'Only in jest.'

'You *are* going to miss me. Our nights of drinking and watching football on TV.'

'I'm not going to miss the snoring. Christ, I thought there were tree fellers outside the other night.'

'Turns out, there was only two of them.' Watt smiled. 'But you better elaborate that my snoring can be heard from the other bedroom or else this pack of hyenas will be all over you. Slip up once, Paddy, and they never let you forget.'

'Shut up. They know we have separate rooms.'

Miller was looking over at Lou's companion.

'Not boring you, are we, Frank?' Percy said.

'What? No, sorry.' He drank some of his own lager.

'I have to admit, she's a good-looking woman,' Gibb said. 'I don't know how your old man does it.'

'He's got a big wallet, obviously. It's not his charm or wit.'

'He must have the gift of the gab,' Watt said.

'Look who's talking,' Gibb said. 'Why else would Kate Murphy be attracted to you? Nay, why else would she have asked you to move in?'

Watt laughed. 'Paddy here's having withdrawal

symptoms. He won't have his best friend around anymore. But you knew this day would come eventually, Paddy. You knew one day I'd grow up and leave the nest.'

'Withdrawal symptoms my arse.'

Just then the door opened and Steffi Walker and Julie Stott walked in.

'Uh oh, here's snitch and snatch. Grab your wallets, lads,' Watt said.

'Thanks, Andy,' Steffi said. 'If you're buying, I'll have a lager. What about you, Julie?'

'Same. Thanks, Andy.'

'Aw, Jesus, me and my big mouth.'

Watt got up as the two female sergeants brought chairs over to the table.

'You two out on the randan?' Gibb asked.

'It's not Friday, sir,' Julie said.

'But we are off duty now, so it's okay to have a drink,' added Steffi, looking sideways at Purcell.

'What you do in your own time, and all that,' Percy said.

'We did just come from the station.' Julie pulled a sheet of paper from her inside pocket as Watt sat down with their drinks. They raised their glasses before Julie carried on.

'We were working late and one of the guys from robbery came over to speak to us. Which is unusual enough, but what he told us next was even more surprising; the watch we found on Adele Mason was reported stolen.'

'Where was it stolen from?'

'The McIver house. As in Gus McIver's house.' Julie looked at Miller. 'The man you arrested for killing his wife.'

'Allegedly killing her. I remember. He has denied the murder to this day and we've never found her body.'

'I'll make a call in the morning,' Percy said. 'Get along to Saughton and speak to him. His lawyer should be there with him. Tell him what we've found but it doesn't mean anything. As in, the Crown Office aren't going to let him go right now.'

'We'll at least talk to him,' Gibb said.

'McIver said the watch was in the house the night she disappeared,' Miller said. 'So how did Adele Mason end up dying with it in her pocket?'

'I'm sure McIver will be keen to tell us,' Steffi said. 'We know the corpse isn't his wife, as they identified Adele through dental records this afternoon. But it's curious why she would have those stolen items on her.'

'Let's keep an open mind, folks,' Purcell said. He looked over at his father. 'He's not got his tongue down her throat just yet. That's always a good sign.'

'Well, I'd better be going,' Watt said.

'Are we keeping you up?' Gibb said.

'You know how it is, Paddy.' He stood up and put his coat on. 'I'll catch the rest of you guys tomorrow.'

'Don't get too pished when you go home. Saughton tomorrow,' Miller said.

'You make that sound like a fun park or something.'

'They play *Don't drop the soap* up there,' Gibb said, looking at his watch.

'Not you as well, Paddy?' Purcell said. 'Leaving me to drink with these reprobates? They'll all be wanting to buy me a drink.'

'Not us,' Steffi said. 'Me and Julie only came in for one.'

'Surely you jest,' Gibb said. 'Call yourselves hardened detectives? Going out with that bus driver has made you soft in the head.'

'He's on backshift and doesn't mind if we go out for a few. 'I'd kick his arse if he did,' Steffi said.

'Right, I'm going,' Watt said. 'You got a minute, Paddy?'

'Uh oh, Paddy's in trouble,' Purcell said.

'Jesus, Andy. That means I need to stand up.'

'Come on, you can do it,' Julie said.

'You, young lady, can put a sock in it,' Gibb said, getting up and following Watt outside.

'Before you start, Andy, I know you took one of my

razor blades. But it's okay. That's why I buy the cheapo throwaways.'

'Listen, mate, I want to say that I appreciate you letting me stay with you for a while, but it's time for me to move on.'

'I know she asked you, but you don't need to feel pressured about moving out.'

'I know that. But the day was going to come eventually.'

Gibb put a hand on Watt's arm. 'We've been through a lot, you and me, so you know you can come and stay anytime. Maggie likes you, despite you taking the piss out of her at times.'

Watt laughed. 'I only do it because I know she can take a joke. She's a good laugh. She should move in full time with you. You're good for each other, Paddy.'

'Her daughter's off to Aberdeen uni and I think it's all been a culture shock for both of them. She's going to come live with me full time soon.'

'Then the timing is perfect. I'm going down to talk to Kate now.'

They walked down to the taxi rank outside the hotel. Watt opened the back door and stepped in. Gibb held the door open. 'Will you be late tonight? I'll probably be in my pyjamas when you get in.'

'That's it, Paddy, make the taxi driver think we're a couple.'

'I won't be able to run your bath later. But listen, try and keep it down when you get to bed. You know I'm a light sleeper.'

'Let the door go.'

'Anyway, you have your own key now. I'll see you later. And don't wake me in the morning like you did this morning.'

'Fuck off, Paddy.'

Gibb laughed and shut the door.

The taxi driver looked in the mirror as he did a U-turn. 'It's okay nowadays, mate. Even for older blokes.'

'Sod off. We're just friends.'

'Sure you are.'

When they were at the lights at St Mary Street, Watt's phone dinged with a text message.

That's for all the times you slagged me off in the pub.

Bastard Watt replied. Then sent a smiley face.

Kate was watching TV when he got to her flat.

He stood in the middle of her living room, smiled and nodded.

'Welcome home,' she said, throwing her arms around him.

TWELVE

'I wasn't here at the time of Gus McIver's arrest,' Jeni Bridge said to Percy Purcell as he sat across from her.

'I wasn't here either, but I had Frank Miller fill me in.'

They were drinking coffee in her office. The sky was the colour of wet concrete. Wind threw itself at the window. Just looking at the sky made Jeni feel cold.

'He's never stopped protesting his innocence, has he?' she said.

'Not one bit. He admitted that they had argued earlier in the week. Two days later, Becky McIver goes missing. Nobody turned up to school to pick the kids up. Gus was called and he said his wife should be there to get them. He left work and picked them up. The following morning, she hadn't come home and he reported her missing.'

'And after an investigation, he was arrested for her murder. Tell me the finer details, Percy.'

So he did.

'Maggie's going to be sad, and no mistake,' Gibb said from the back seat.

'What? Don't talk pish, Paddy.' Andy Watt sat in the front of the car as Miller drove.

'At least she'll get peace and quiet now,' Miller said as he pulled into the car park of Saughton Prison on the west side of Edinburgh. 'Although the same can't be said for Kate Murphy.'

'Jesus,' Gibb said. 'Imagine waking up to Andy clambering all over you.'

'I thought you said he did that to *you*,' Miller laughed.

'Shut your hole, Miller. And keep that engine running while I finish my fag.'

A few minutes later with the cigarette finished and the next one already being thought about, the three detectives walked inside the prison and were shown to one of the interview rooms.

Gus McIver's lawyer, Richard Sullivan, was already sitting at the table with McIver.

'You've got some balls showing up here, Miller,' McIver said.

'Your hair's got more grey,' Miller said, sitting on one of the chairs opposite the prisoner.

'We can just as easily piss off from here,' Gibb said. 'We're doing this as a courtesy to you, so put a zipper on it.' He and Watt sat down next to Miller.

'My client appreciates you coming,' Sullivan said, shooting McIver a look. The prisoner made a face.

'Let's go through your story again, McIver,' Miller said.

Gus McIver was forty-nine years old, with short grey hair. He didn't look like the typical university professor.

His fingers were tapping the table in front of him and it seemed as if all the air had left him. He looked at Sullivan before starting.

'Yeah. I already told you Becky and I went at it all the time. Everybody knew that. She always said I was an arsehole, but I was *her* arsehole. Know what I mean?'

Sullivan nodded.

'We found blood in the bathtub,' Gibb said, already irritated with the man.

'And as you are well aware, I told you she must have had a nose bleed and the blood got in there. I mean, it was a minuscule amount they found. It wasn't a blood bath. If you see what I mean.'

'Tell us about the watch,' Miller said.

'First, you have to understand Becky; she lived for going to parties. Dressing up in her best garb. Some of my colleagues had friends in high places and she loved going to the society parties. She came from money, but you knew that. She loved rubbing shoulders with some of Edinburgh's wealthy. You know the sort; lots of money but with the intelligence of a stick. Her father was like that. Mister Big Shot. She took after him.

'The day she disappeared, I got a call at work that the kids hadn't been picked up from school. When I got home, there was no sign of her.'

'You were having an affair with a student,' Gibb said. 'Pretty convenient, your wife going missing. It opened the door for you having it away with that wee lassie.'

'She was not a *wee lassie*, as you so eloquently put it. She was a very mature twenty-one-year-old. And if I may remind you, the legal age in Scotland is sixteen.' McIver sat back in his chair.

'It still provides motive,' Miller said. 'You wanted your wife out of the way, so you could move the student in with you.'

McIver sat forward again and Miller could see why some students might have found him intimidating.

'Move in? My God, man, I have two kids. I was hardly going to have her move in with me.'

'Again; still motive. Why would we believe you weren't planning on moving your relationship forward?' Gibb said.

'Relationship? Who speaks like that? You the dinosaur contingent?'

'Cheeky bastard,' Gibb said. 'You remember what side your bread is buttered on.'

McIver turned to Sullivan. 'Sounds like a veiled threat to me.'

'There's nothing fucking veiled about it, McIver,' Gibb said, his face going red with anger. 'We came here as a courtesy. To give you the benefit of the doubt, if there was any. But we can just as easily dismiss this out of hand.'

McIver looked between his lawyer and the detectives.

'I mean this in the best possible way, Gus, but shut it,' Sullivan said. 'Tell them the facts and quit taking the piss or else they will indeed be out of here and you will be, in no uncertain terms, fucked.'

'Why didn't you just say so?' McIver said. He looked at Gibb. 'Look, I'm sorry. My nerves have been shot since I found out that Adele was found murdered.'

'You knew Adele Mason?' Watt said, hoping Paddy didn't drop down of heart failure.

'Of course I did. She was a babysitter for me and my wife.'

Gibb looked at Miller before turning his attention back to McIver. 'You didn't tell us that before.'

McIver shrugged. 'I don't mean to sound like a know-it-all, but you didn't ask. It was usually Becky's sister Dee who would babysit the kids. But sometimes she couldn't, so we got Adele.'

'When was the last time Adele Mason looked after your kids?' Miller said.

'You think I was sleeping with her, too, don't you?' McIver said.

'I didn't say that.'

'It's in your tone. But let me tell you, I wouldn't touch her with yours. She was around sixteen, seventeen at the time, but what a mouth on her. And opinions! Jesus, could that girl talk for Scotland. If yakking was an Olympic sport, she'd be on top of the podium. Right little fucking madam she was. She was going to take on the world. Save the whales, paint the world pink, and ride a unicorn to work.'

'How long did she babysit for?' Watt said.

'Maybe six months. She only came round if Dee couldn't do it. But then Adele said she couldn't do it anymore. Thank God. I had already started looking for somebody else. I didn't want her promising my daughter she'd get a pony for her birthday one day, instead of getting a car. Tree-hugger didn't begin to describe her. I was a little bit scared of her, truth be told.'

'You think she was dangerous?' Watt said.

'No, not dangerous. More... passionate. Bordering on the loony. She would get excited when she was talking about saving some obscure little cactus or something. There was just something in her eyes. I told Becky about this, but she dismissed it out of hand. It was yet another thing we argued about.'

'How was her relationship with your wife?' Gibb asked, still smarting over the *dinosaur* remark.

'Fine. Becky wasn't jealous of Adele if that's what you mean.'

'When Adele was babysitting, did your wife know of your little indiscretions with other women?'

'Yes, of course. We both had other partners. If she suspected I was sleeping with Adele, she didn't voice it. But there was no way I was interested in Adele that way.'

Miller looked at him. 'We went over your statement, and it says that you *suspected* your wife was having an affair. You couldn't give us a name. Unless you can supply one now?'

'Well.... no, but obviously I knew the signs. I was doing the same thing, remember? We both knew we played away from home, but this was different with her. It was like he was her boyfriend rather than a bit of fun. She was staying out late, not answering her phone, or talking on her phone in the bathroom. I heard her laughing in there one night, shortly before she went missing and I heard her tell him *I love you*. Now, I don't know about you DI Miller, but I get a little bit suspicious when I hear my wife say that on the phone.'

'And we might have been able to verify that if her phone had been found after she disappeared,' Watt said. 'It was switched off or destroyed. Whatever happened to it, it stopped pinging off mobile phone towers.'

'She wouldn't have left that behind. Or her precious watch or those rings. Those were family heir-looms. But as I said, they were there, because your crime scene people photographed them, and then they were gone.'

'You could have taken them, Mr McIver.'

'But I didn't. And you lot know that. If you remember, I wasn't allowed back in after you got it into your head that I had killed her. It went from a missing person case to murder in the blink of an eye. Her sister put a stick in the spokes, didn't she? And when I saw those photos, there was the bloody watch on the dresser. And then when I was told to stay out, you posted a uniform at the door. Then the forensics people came back to take more prints and photos.

Especially photos of the en suite bathroom where the blood drops were. So they photographed the bedroom again. More photos. And low and behold, the watch was gone.'

'It didn't just disappear,' Gibb said.

'That's what I've just been saying.' He stopped short of insulting Gibb again. 'If I wasn't allowed back in, then how did they disappear? Becky must have come back and taken them.'

'How did she get past the uniform at the door?'

'I have no idea. Oh, wait; maybe she used her key,' he said in a sarcastic tone.

Sullivan threw him a look and McIver sat forward again. 'Look, she could have got in the back door, taken the stuff she was most fond of and left again. That copper at the front door wouldn't have known if an elephant had been in there. Besides, wasn't he sitting in a car with his partner?'

Gibb looked at Miller, who nodded the affirmative.

McIver carried on. 'They were in the car so even if Becky had made a noise, they wouldn't have heard her. There's a door in the wall at the side of the house, and there's a door into the house on that side. Becky could have slipped in and nobody would have seen her.'

'This is all very subjective,' Gibb said. 'For all we know, you might have given Adele Mason those items.'

'Oh what? Seriously? Now we're back to me taking

them? I'm telling you, somebody came back to get them after they were on the dresser. I just told you, I was in the station helping you with your enquiries when that forensic crew went back in. They were there when the first photos were taken, and I wasn't out of anybody's sight. Me and the kids were staying over at Dee's house that night. Their door was double-locked and I didn't have a key. Which didn't bode well if the house went on fire. So I didn't leave. Then you lot brought me to the station where I was interviewed, the forensics took more photos and the items were missing. I can't make it clearer to you; I didn't take the watch and rings, and I didn't kill Becky.'

'You're saying she left without her kids?' Watt said.

'That's exactly what I'm saying. Women have killed their kids to be with their lover. Becky just left. She could have been wanting to go with him to start a new life. It happens. And nobody believes me.'

There was silence in the room for a moment. Then Sullivan spoke up.

'I'm presenting this to the court today. Or having somebody else present it. But the point is, I want my client released on license while this mess is sorted.'

'That's up to you,' Gibb said.

'Meantime, please make sure you do a thorough investigation into how that young woman came to be in possession of Mrs McIver's belongings.'

Another few minutes of talk and then the detectives were ready to leave.

'He has a bloody good point,' Gibb said, lighting up as soon as they were back in the car.

'What do you think, Frank?' Watt said as Miller started the car.

'I agree with Paddy. I think McIver was set up. But by who? Adele Mason? What reason would she have?'

'Let's find out,' Gibb said, blowing smoke around the car.

'Jesus, Paddy,' Watt said. 'Usually, when you blow smoke out your arse, it isn't as cloying as this.'

'Shut up. You should have started smoking years ago. You wouldn't be squealing like a wee lassie now.'

Miller drove the car out of the prison car park.

THIRTEEN

'Come on, Sparky, get a move on,' Roaster said to himself and looked at his watch, starting to get agitated. Then he looked up and saw his friend come into the bar. 'Christ, I thought you had bailed.'

'Fucking bus driver. He saw me in his mirror, shut the door, and fucked off. I was running and shouting and everything. Wanker.'

'Never mind that. Tidy yourself up a bit. You've got sweat on your face and it's October. You don't want the women to think you started without them.'

'Fuck sake. I'm out of breath. If I ever see that bastard driving a bus again, I'll—'

'What? Give him a stern talking to?'

'Kick his bawbag for him,' Sparky said.

'It might have been a lassie. Besides, if you only

saw the back of the bus as it pulled away, how would you recognise him?'

Sparky took his pint from the bar and chugged half it down. 'Let me just get it off my chest, for God's sake.'

'Okay, Don Corleone.'

'Fuck you. It cost me fifteen quid on a bastard taxi.'

'I hope you brought some extra cash to splash on the ladies?' Roaster said, a worried frown now on his face. 'The last time we overspent on a pair of judies, I had to sub you thirty quid, and I saw fuck all of that back.'

'I made it up by paying for the Ruby Murray after that.'

'The one you blew all over the back seat of that taxi afterwards.' Roaster laughed.

Sparky grinned. 'That driver was ragin'. But my arse was on fire for a week after that. Those manky bastards in that restaurant. Even the rats blow chunks after eating in there.'

'If they don't make it into the pot, that is.'

'Jesus. You're starting to make me feel ill again.' Sparky made a face and drank more of his lager.

'Right, get a grip. Here they come. And tuck your shirt in, Christ.' Roaster put his pint on the bar and rubbed his hands together. '*Dolly* and *Babe*, aka, Skye and Poppy.'

'Do you call Skye *Dolly* because she has big tits like *Dolly Parton*?'

Roaster looked at his friend and shook his head. 'No, I call her that because she looks like a fucking sheep. Seriously. Have a word with yourself.'

'Why do you call Poppy *Babe*?'

'Because she's a pig.'

'A pig with money.'

'Now he gets it.'

'That's why we're courting them.' Sparky grinned, and if there was such a thing as an invisible lightbulb, it would have lit up above his head at that moment.

'Don't say *courting*, moron. We don't want them to think that you're an eighty-year-old trapped in a thirty-year-old's body.'

'Twenty-nine and three quarters.'

'Just don't open your mouth and spout some pish.' Roaster smiled as Skye came up to him.

She and Poppy were in their forties. *Bored divorcees* she had told them when the men had bumped into them in the bar. It was a secluded place in the basement of a hotel in the New Town, that catered to individuals who wanted discretion. A singles place for those of a mature nature. *For the oldies who wanted to bag off with somebody*.

'Hello, handsome,' she said. Her lipstick was red

and luscious. She had loosened her coat and was smiling at him.

'Hello, honey. What you for?'

'The usual, please.'

'Take your coats off and Sparky will check them for you.' He knew this was a ploy on the hotel's part; check the coats, make them feel like they were going to be staying here longer.

The ladies took their coats off and Poppy kissed Sparky before he scuttled away.

'Poppy, my love, the usual for you too?'

'Thank you, sweetheart,' she said, grinning her over-bite grin.

Roaster held up a finger and got the barman's attention. An older bloke with an ill-fitting toupee that made him look like he'd cut out a piece of carpet and shoved it on at the last minute. Maybe the management didn't want him flirting with the patrons, although Roaster couldn't imagine what sort of woman would want to flirt with the man. He looked like his idea of having a good time with a woman was following her in his car with the headlights off.

'You got them in?' Sparky whispered to Roaster as he came back.

'What took so long? Were you raking about in their fucking pockets again?'

'I was looking for a mint the last time, I told you.'

'Anyway, I've already ordered two G&Ts and a couple of Bells. And it's your round,' he reminded Sparky.

'Of course it is. I hope they're going to get a round in.'

'Shut up, they'll fucking hear you.' He had a quick sideways glance and saw the women had moved away and were sitting at a table by the back wall.

'Good. I told them last time not to sit too close to that old nob who plays the shitey music,' Sparky said.

'More popularly known as the DJ.'

'Last time, I almost had to use semaphore just to hold a conversation.'

'Can you stop moaning for a minute?' Roaster grinned and lifted his pint and two of the smaller glasses as he looked at the ladies.

Sparky held out his hand for the change. 'Jesus, you would think we could keep the fucking glasses at these prices.'

'Again, smile and make polite conversation. Don't forget the big picture at the end of the day.'

'That's why I'm here. But this is the last time, Roaster, I mean it.'

'Aye, aye, whatever.' He took a sip of his drink. 'Besides, I don't think the boss would be very happy if we just decided we don't want a part of this anymore. I don't think we have a choice.'

FOURTEEN

'Look at this!' Lord Snooty held up a dress in front of him.

'It doesn't look like it would fit you,' Princess said.

'For you, I mean! Here, try it on!' He laughed and threw it at her.

She batted it away and it fell on the floor. 'Stop arsing around. Get the jewellery, donkey.' She laughed at him, despite herself.

'Aw, c'mon. If it doesn't fit you, it might fit me.' He grinned like an idiot.

'Oh, I would pay money to see that.'

She turned towards the vanity that was against the wall and sat down on the seat in front of the mirrors. Imagined the woman who would normally sit there. The room was in darkness except for the thin shafts of LED light, cutting through the unlit room.

'I believe there are a couple of Rolex watches in there,' Snooty said, pointing to the box with his torch.

Princess opened the jewellery box but it was full of rings. 'Wrong. These are mine.'

'Where are the watches then? There's a cheapo Submariner and—'

'Hardly cheapo.'

Snooty held up his hands, the light dancing around. 'Point taken, but it's the GMT Master II that I'm interested in. Red and blue ceramic dial in white gold.'

She opened a drawer and moved things about until she saw a wooden box. She took it out and placed it on the top of the vanity. The two Rolex watches sat inside.

'Ooh, me likey,' Snooty said, taking the box from her. He had gloves on and was tempted to take one off to fondle the metal strap but knew it would be foolish to do that. He let the light bounce off the faces then beamed a smile at her. 'There are more. I think me and the boys should divvy them up between us.'

'That's on you. If you get caught with it on, you'll get nailed.'

'Ach, you worry too much. I love watches. I wear a decent one at work, but these babies, they're the biz.'

'Our friends will not be happy about you keeping them.'

'If we take one each, then what's the problem?' Snooty was like a child in a toy shop.

'They want the cash. We have a buyer lined up. This can go sideways very quickly unless we screw the nut.'

Princess put the rings into the pillow case she was using, and then started going through more drawers. More boxes, more necklaces, rings, and a couple of female luxury watches.

Snooty closed the lid of the Rolex box and put it into the pillow case that was lying on the bed.

'Come on then, our job here is done,' he said.

'Let's just rough the place up a little more.'

'Now that I'm happy to do.'

FIFTEEN

They were sitting in the conference room, rain battering off the windows. Jeni Bridge was drinking coffee. 'I'm introducing a new smoking policy; I think we should be able to smoke in here. Who's with me?'

Paddy Gibb's hand shot up like he'd felt a jolt of electricity shooting through his chair.

Percy Purcell, Andy Watt, and Frank Miller grimaced and kept their hands down. Steffi Walker and Julie Stott too.

'Jesus, this is a conspiracy. However, being commander of the Edinburgh contingent, I can over-rule you all.'

'Technically, no, but if nobody else in the station minds getting spattered with rain and shivering like they had some disease, then don't let us stop you.'

'God, Percy. The one person who I thought would

have thrown me a life belt if I was drowning.' Jeni was holding a packet in her hand, still on the fence. 'What's your thoughts on this, DCI Gibb?'

Fuck them all. 'Considering how stressful this job is, and how it was good enough in the old days, I don't see the harm.'

Watt looked at him. 'That's what Kate will be thinking as she lifts your lungs out to weigh them after she's cut you open.'

'Aw, fu... for goodness sake. Drama queen or what?'

'Fine. Go ahead. But I for one want the window open. I don't want to be sucking in your smelly air,' Miller said.

'Back in the seventies, you would have been shoved into a locker just for saying that out loud.'

'You've been watching too much TV. You and I both started in the eighties,' Watt said.

Gibb shrugged and took a cigarette out of the packet. Like drawing back a spear and waiting for the order to throw it.

Meantime, Jeni had cracked a window and had lit up. 'My ex-husband is the chief constable. If anybody has any complaints, I'm sure he'll take great delight in tearing a strip off me.'

Gibb had his lighter out in a flash. 'Just for moral support,' he said.

Jeni sat down. 'Now, yesterday's interview with Gus McIver. Let's recap.'

'He once again went into great detail about how the crime scene team went back to his house when he was out and the watch and other items were missing,' Miller said. 'He couldn't have gone back and taken them because he was at the station helping us with our enquiries.'

'Nobody believed him, including the jury,' Jeni replied. 'They did indeed go missing, so who took them?'

'Nobody knows,' Gibb said. 'The family were interviewed but nobody knows anything.'

'What family members does he have left?'

'His two kids, who are living with his wife's only sibling; a sister: Dee Raeburn. McIver doesn't have anybody else.'

'I'm assuming the sister was interviewed?' Jeni said, tapping ash into a paper cup.

'She was,' Miller said. 'She had an alibi for the day Becky McIver went missing.'

'What happened with his house?' Steffi asked.

'It's being held in trust for when the kids are old enough to own it. Becky McIver's family had money, so the house was paid off,' Gibb replied. 'There's no mortgage on it.'

'How was their relationship?' Julie asked.

'Like any other couple; they had their ups and downs,' Miller said. 'But Dee told us that Becky had mentioned that she knew about her husband having an affair.'

'And he denies having an affair with Adele Mason?'

'Yes. She was strictly his babysitter,' Miller said. 'According to McIver they had an open marriage, rather than just them cheating on each other. But he seems to think his wife had entered into a relationship with another man.'

Purcell sat up straighter in his chair as Jeni stubbed her cigarette out. 'If he is indeed innocent, we need to find out who took the jewellery that was found on Adele. So, we should start with who had access to the house.'

'Yes, let's start there, Percy,' Jeni said. 'I also want her boyfriend found. *Lord Snooty.*' She stood up. 'Right, let's get at it before Paddy decides to crash a can of Carly Spesh to go with his ciggie.'

SIXTEEN

'I suppose he told you he wasn't sleeping with Adele Mason?' Dee Raeburn said. She showed the detectives into her living room. Then she stopped abruptly and gestured for Miller and Watt to sit down.

They sat next to each other on the settee while Dee stood looking at them.

'We're just going over the background again,' Miller said.

'Why? Why now? Because of that little tramp being found dead? If he wasn't locked up, I would say he had murdered her too.'

It hadn't been revealed publicly about the watch being found on her, but Miller didn't think that would remain a secret for long. The YouTubers had been warned not to reveal that detail but he didn't hold out much hope.

'She was linked to your brother-in-law, yes,' Watt said. 'Only because she was a babysitter for them.'

At last Dee sat down. 'Babysitter? She was all round whore, sergeant. Young Adele had a reputation for sleeping with older men. I don't doubt for one second he was giving her one.' She looked at them. 'You want coffee?'

'No thanks,' Miller replied for both of them. 'What makes you so sure he was sleeping with her?'

'Becky told me. She found used condoms in the bathroom. She was on the pill and they didn't use condoms. Becky thought he was coming home and sleeping with Adele when they were both supposed to be out.'

'Do you think Adele had anything to do with your sister's disappearance?'

'Who knows? I didn't like her. I only met her a few times. Cocky little bitch, so she was. Typical of somebody who comes from money; it's like Victorian times all over again. What would her motive have been though?'

'So she could have Becky's husband all to herself,' Watt said.

'She was just a teenager back then, if I remember correctly.'

'She was. Still, some teenagers do strange things for love.'

'Let me ask you, inspector; do you believe McIver is innocent?'

'As a law enforcement officer, I can't speculate on that.'

Watt sat up straighter. 'We obviously know that McIver was in prison when Adele was murdered, so we have to find out who else would want to harm her.'

'It's a shame she went down that road. Disrespecting her father the way she did. She was a smart girl and could have done anything she wanted with her life. What a waste.'

'She had a friend who she called *Lord Snooty*. Have you ever heard of anybody by that name?'

'As I said, I haven't seen her for years. God knows what would have become of my brother-in-law had he continued his relationship with that girl. But he's in the right place.'

'You believe he killed your sister?' Miller said.

'Of course I do. Women don't just walk out on their children. She left everything behind and there's been no sight of her since.'

'Some women do,' Watt said.

'What?' Dee looked at him like he'd brought something in on the sole of his shoe.

'Some women leave it all behind to go with a lover. Some even kill their kids. It does happen. They leave everything behind to start from scratch. They're not in a good mental state when they do that, but it happens.'

'My sister did not leave her kids behind. He killed her and her body is out there somewhere.'

SEVENTEEN

'Nice place you have here, Richard,' Gus McIver said, looking out the living room window across the Forth to Fife.

'It was, until the press decided to camp outside my building.'

'Well, they all think the mass-murdering child killer is living in your flat now.'

'You're going to have to leave in the boot of one of our cars,' Tai Lopez – now Mrs Tai Sullivan – said as she handed McIver a soft drink.

'When you've spent the best part of six years in a little cell waiting to have your head kicked in, then riding in the boot of a car is nothing. Cheers.'

'Make sure that's all you drink,' Sullivan said. 'No alcohol, part of the license agreement.'

McIver grinned. 'I'm used to not having a drink.

Being on the outside is more important. I can't wait to see the kids again.'

Sullivan turned to him so fast that McIver thought the man was going to assault him. 'Don't even fucking start with that again. You have not to set foot near the kids. If I find out that you have even called them, I'll be on the phone to that fucking judge so fast you'll think you've been teleported back to Saughton. Do I make myself clear?'

'Jesus, Dickie, take it easy. If you had an aortic aneurysm, it would have exploded by now. I just said I can't wait to see the kids, but I meant when you prove me innocent.'

Sullivan turned away from the man, now having doubts about what he had done. 'Step out of line once, and I will help them hang you. I'm your lawyer and your friend, but I can be your worst enemy.'

'God, Dickie, I've spoken to drama students who were less dramatic.' He sat down on one of the leather chairs. 'You have to understand, I've been locked up for so long, I can barely remember how a telephone works.'

'Let's keep it that way.'

'Frankly, I'm surprised they went for it,' McIver said. 'I mean, it was a long shot, but you pulled it off. As far as they know, I might be guilty and I'm going to disappear into the sunset. How do they know I won't?'

'Because I told them, if you did, I'd hunt you down

myself. And by the time I'm finished, you won't have to worry about being in a cell.'

'It's scary when you say it in that tone.'

Sullivan turned back to look at him. 'Take it seriously. I know people. In my line of work, you get to meet some bad bastards. Some of them owe me a favour.'

'I thought we were friends. I'm beginning to have doubts.'

'I'm your lawyer first, your friend second.' His phone dinged letting him know a text message had arrived. He read it and replied.

'Technically called a solicitor.'

'But we still call ourselves lawyers, so as not to confuse the great unwashed.' Sullivan looked at the other man. 'You're staying here because I made a promise to the judge. Norma Banks is going to be pissed off when she hears, because she was against it, but luckily for us, there are higher powers than her.'

'I still wouldn't want to mess with her.'

'Good. Keep that thought. Her daughter's on her way up here now. She also happens to be DI Frank Miller's wife.'

'What? You really are trying to upset me, Dickie. I will not be best pleased if that woman comes in here and starts harassing me.'

The doorbell rang and Sullivan went to answer it. A couple of minutes later, Kim Smith walked in.

'Kim Smith, this is Angus McIver. Kim is an investigator with the Procurator Fiscal's office.'

McIver stood up, beaming. He held a hand out for her to shake. 'Frank Miller's wife, eh? I must say, it takes all sorts. I won't ask what you see in him, but if he ever dumps you for a younger woman...'

Kim didn't shake his hand. 'I'm here to talk to you, Mr McIver, not apply for the role of trophy wife.'

'Spunky too. I like it. But don't let this look fool you; this is just my prison look. You know, that certain look a man takes on after being in a cell for six years. That certain smell and aura he has about him.'

'*Feral* by Ralph Lauren,' Kim said.

'Now you're getting it.' McIver grinned. 'Say, Dickie, how about putting the kettle on?'

Kim walked through to the kitchen with Sullivan, where they found Tai making a sandwich.

'Hi, Kim. How's business?'

'Great. I'm back into the swing of it. How about you? How's the restaurant coming along?'

'Better, now that I've found a new manager to help me run the place.'

'You need more time to yourselves now that you're married.'

'We're trying for a baby too.' She smiled at Kim.

'That's wonderful!' She hugged Tai.

'How are your little girls?'

'Annie sleeps right through the night. Emma loves helping with her new sister. I couldn't be happier.'

'How's the paparazzi crowd downstairs?' Sullivan asked.

'Baying for blood.'

'I already told McIver that he will have to go out of here in the boot.'

'You can call me Gus!' McIver shouted through from the living room.

'My dad's department is taking charge of looking after him,' Kim said. 'I'm liaising with them. I'll be his nanny until we get this sorted out.'

'And nobody argues with Neil McGovern,' Sullivan replied.

'Not a second time. But there are several properties around Edinburgh where he'll be safe if we have to move him at short notice. I can have backup, but I'll be team leader.'

'Team leader? You mean babysitter?'

'That's not the official term, but more or less. I used to work with my father's department as you know, so it made sense to bring me on board since I'm with the PF's office now. Jack Miller works with my dad, too, so he'll be helping.'

'It makes sense,' Tai said. 'Frank's father is a retired

detective, so I can't think of anybody else better for the job. It frees up manpower.'

'Still talking about me, I see,' McIver said from the living room.

They walked out and stood in front of him. 'It's for your own safety,' Sullivan said.

'And I've never felt safer, Dickie.'

'Don't get too cocky,' Kim said. 'Not everybody believes you're innocent.'

'Well, that's nice.'

'You'll be glad to hear we're going for a little ride,' Kim said. Then she turned to Sullivan. 'One of the conditions was me getting a key to your apartment since you wanted him to come and stay here.'

'Here it is,' Tai said, taking it out of her pocket and handing it over.

'Don't worry, I won't let him in here on his own. I'll be with him until you get back if we come in.'

'As you know, my office is literally across the road, so it will be easy for me to come over. Tai works in her restaurant some nights, but otherwise, she's out in the afternoons.'

'Fine. Let's get going, Mr McIver,' Kim said.

'Where are we going?'

'You'll find out. And don't worry, the Range Rover I'm driving has limousine tint on the back windows.

Designed not to let flash photography through. They won't even know you're in there.'

McIver stood up and smiled. 'Great. Let's get going.'

'Oh, and one more thing; if you ditch me, I'll find you and teach you a lesson you won't forget.'

'Fair enough. But you must be brave, having a suspected murderer sitting in the back seat of the car.'

'I worked for a government department and I trained with army special forces. One finger on me, Gus, and I will tear you into little pieces. That I promise you.'

'I'm not a murderer – I was just saying.' He looked across at Sullivan who shot him a *don't fuck with her* look.

'Let's go, Gus,' Kim said.

EIGHTEEN

'These apartments are actually fantastic,' Jean Melrose said to George Stone as he was showing her around. The hard hat felt heavy on her head but it was a necessity since this was a work area.

'They're going to be first class, especially after you've added your touch to them, Jean. I'm glad Molloy brought you on board.'

They were looking out of one of the back windows of the main building, across to where the exclusive townhouses were going to be built.

She turned to him. 'My father told me there were prisoners of war housed here during the second world war.'

'This school for the deaf has quite a background. This is one instance where I wish walls would talk.'

'I spoke to my assistant and the staging can go ahead as soon as the walls are dry,' Jean said as they left the apartment and went into the main corridor. There were men going about the work, painting and finishing.

'That would be magic. I had some clown working for me before, but she's gone now.'

Jean smiled. She knew Stone was crude and a bit of a misogynist, but he was part of Robert Molloy's consortium, and they threw a lot of money her way. Not only did her company get to stage the show homes, but she designed the custom interiors for the affluent buyers.

'There you are!' a man said to her as he reached the top of the grand staircase.

Jean turned to Stone. 'It's my stepson.' She looked at Adam Melrose. 'What are you doing here? Is anything wrong with the girls?'

'Can we talk in private?'

Stone looked at her. 'I'll see you downstairs.' He walked away, ignoring Melrose.

'We can talk in one of the apartments.'

'You're damn straight we can talk.'

They went back into the apartment she had just left with Stone. 'What's the matter, Adam?'

'You know, when I was a little boy and you married my dad, I was happy. I was getting another mum back in my life. I even liked the little girl you had. A little sister I now had. Life was good, but when you divorced, that turned my life upside down.'

Jean smelled the drink on his breath. 'Adam, why don't I come around to your place tonight and we can talk then. Give you a chance to sober up.'

'Oh no, we'll talk now. Or rather, I'm going to talk and you're going to listen.' He paced round what was going to be the living room of the new apartment. He suddenly stopped. 'I didn't go with my dad down to London, but your little daughter did. Then she came back to Edinburgh and you took her in before she died. You took the little junkie girl in because she was your flesh and blood and that trumps everything doesn't it?'

'You're talking through drink.'

'Bollocks! You took her in but you didn't know what my father was like. Dealing bloody drugs. And she was getting involved in that shit too. And you wonder why I don't bring my little girls round to see you? I don't want them in that environment!'

'Good God, it's not as if *I'm* a drug dealer!'

'But you let that little whore back into your life. And now I have no choice but to let my little girls see you because of that fucking boyfriend of yours.'

'What are you talking about?'

'Don't play the innocent with me!'

'I really don't know what you're talking about.'

'You despicable old bitch!' Melrose grabbed her by the arm just as two men walked in, followed by Stone. One of the men tackled Melrose and took him down. He screamed and shouted while the second man went through his pockets and took the car keys out.

'Sorry about this, Jean,' Stone said, 'but he nearly knocked one of my men down. And that wouldn't have had a happy ending.'

'Oh, George, I thought he was going to hit me.'

'Nobody's going to touch you. One of my men will be with you at all times for the rest of the day and I'm sure Robert will have somebody escorting you from tomorrow.' He put an arm around her shoulder. 'You're safe now, love.'

The two men hauled Melrose to his feet and dragged him out of the apartment. 'You haven't heard the last of this!' Melrose shouted.

'I'll call Robert and let him know what happened,' Stone said.

'No, please, don't do that. It will be better if it comes from me.'

'Fair enough. My men will take him home, and he can pick up his car keys tomorrow from the security office.' The office was a cabin on site, manned twenty-four hours.

'Thank you.' She started crying. Why had her life changed so much? First, her little girl had died, and now her son was against her.

She wondered where it was all going to end.

NINETEEN

Skye wrapped her arms around herself. 'It's a violation. I feel like I was... touched.'

The robbery detective, a surly sergeant who looked like he doubled as a football hooligan, nodded.

'That's the general reaction we get when people have had their homes broken into.' He looked at the female detective he was with and she nodded at him; *drama queen*.

'Just be thankful you weren't here when they broke in. It's better they get in, take your stuff, and leave.' She was standing away from her partner, looking around.

'Our uniformed colleagues who took the initial report said you were out at the time. I know you gave a statement but we'd like to go through everything again, if you don't mind.'

'That's fine.' Skye sat down on a chair. Sergeant

Hooligan sat on the couch while the female officer stayed standing. 'My colleague here is going to look around at the room the things were taken from.'

Skye nodded. The detective's tone made it sound like she didn't have a choice.

'Can you tell me where you were at the time the robbery occurred?'

Skye looked at him, the wheels going round in her head. 'My friend and I were having a drink in a little bar in a hotel in Darnaway Street in the New Town.'

'The singles club?'

Skye managed to look offended. 'Why do you say that?'

'We were there one time when a room got broken into. I haven't frequented the place myself, but, you know...'

'Desperate bints like me have to go there for a man?'

'I'm not saying that. I'm just stating that there's a singles club there in the basement bar.'

'Yes, well, we were at the club. But with our boyfriends.' Skye instantly regretted the term as soon as she'd spoken the words. 'Well, not boyfriends, exactly. Just friends.'

'Who were you there with?'

'My friend, Poppy. We met a couple of guys a few weeks ago and we meet up with them. You know, if you were to go there regularly, you would see the same faces. It's like meeting up with friends.'

'Friends with benefits?'

'Benefits being having a laugh and a few drinks? Then, yes.'

'Who are the boyfriends you meet there?' The detective wasn't there to spare her feelings.

'As I just said, not boyfriends, but friends who are boys. Young men, I mean, not high school seniors. And we don't know where they live. We just meet up, have a laugh and a few drinks.'

'They have names though, I assume?'

'If you mean names that are printed on their birth certificates, then yes. But if you mean names they gave to us, then no. Oh, of course they told us their names, but it could have been Lee Harvey Oswald and Lord Lucan and it wouldn't have made a difference. A lot of people go there because they're cheating on their wives. Or husbands.'

'You married?' Detective Hooligan asked.

'Was. He was a lot older than me and his enthusiasm was stronger than his heart. He died and left me this house and a pile of money in the bank. Some people suggested I married him for his money. He was twenty years older than me, with thinning hair and teeth that could have been replaced by false ones. I didn't marry him for looks.'

'We see that a lot; gold diggers who marry older blokes for their money.'

'Cheeky sod. Did you miss the class on how to interview somebody or something?' Skye managed to look indignant.

'I'm not here to massage your ego. I deal with people who would split my skull with a pickaxe. We're trying to establish some names here.'

'It's just a couple of guys.'

'Did you leave the bar with them?' Hooligan asked.

'Yes.'

'Finally. We're getting somewhere.' He had his notebook out in front of him and was taking notes. 'Where did you go?'

'Up to a flat in Longstone.'

'Slumming it a bit, isn't it? Bit of rough, were they?'

'A bit of fun, more like. They're great boys. They bought us drinks and something to eat from the chippy on the way home, and then we had some fun.'

'Did you all go to the same house at the same time?'

'What's that got to do with it?'

'I want to know if either of them left,' Hooligan said.

'You think one of them might have come here and robbed me? Even if one of them did leave, I don't think he would do that. But no, they didn't leave our sight all night. We went back to a flat, had some fun, and then me and Poppy shared a taxi home. She came in for a nightcap and we found the place had been turned over.'

'How long did it take for the taxi to get here from the time you left?'

'Well, I thought we were going to be watching an in-flight movie, the direction he was taking, but we came straight here from Longstone.'

'Not enough time for them to have beaten you here, robbed you then left. Although I've met some quick workers in my time, I don't think that's realistic in this case. But I'll need their names and the address.'

Skye looked unsure of herself. 'You know how it is when you've had a few. You're in the back of a taxi, canoodling a bit, and the next thing you know, you're at the address. I couldn't tell you where it is.'

'What about when you left? What location did you give the taxi company?'

'They know from the number. When you call them, they know where you're at. Besides, my friend called the taxi company.'

'It was his flat you were in?' Hooligan asked.

'Well, it belonged to *one* of them. I just don't know.'

'You were taking a risk, going home with two strange men.' Hooligan didn't look too impressed. He'd been out with mates before and picked up a couple of old boilers.

'We've known them for a little while. It wasn't the first time we've been back to the flat with them.'

'Anything stick out, that you remember?'

'He wasn't a hunchback if that's what you mean.'

'It isn't. I meant locations. Petrol station, supermarket, something like that.'

'I just know we passed the bus depot on the way to his flat.'

'Lothian Buses, Longstone?'

'If you say so.'

'Anything else?' Hooligan asked.

'Nothing my gin-fuelled brain can remember.'

'How about anything your boyfriends told you about themselves? Like where they work, what car they drive, whether they were married before. Anything like that.'

There was a silence between them for a moment. 'I never thought about this before, but I actually know nothing about them at all. Nothing. The things you mentioned. I don't know where they work, or any personal details about them.'

'How long have you been seeing them?'

'About four weeks or so. They never came back here. We always went to Longstone.' She looked at

Hooligan. 'You don't think they had anything to do with this, do you?'

'I can't speculate.' He stood up as his colleague came back into the room. 'If there's anything else you remember, please give us a call.' He handed her a business card and left the house.

TWENTY

Robert Molloy was in his office in the hotel.

'Business is booming,' Michael Molloy said, coming into the office.

'Don't you ever knock?'

'Why? What were you doing? Watching *Baywatch* on your own again?'

'Don't get smart with me, Michael. And pour us a drink.'

Michael marched across to the drinks cabinet and poured his father a whisky. 'I won't bother. I'm taking Liz out for a meal tonight, and I don't want to be throwing my ring all over the table. You, on the other hand, are a sad old git who will be staying in with his girlfriend, holding hands on the settee, watching *East-Enders*. So you can afford to get pished in the afternoon.'

'Sit down and shut up,' Robert said, accepting the glass from his son. He sat at his desk while Michael sat on the leather settee.

'Jesus, what's got into you?'

Robert savoured the whisky before putting the glass down. 'That job I asked Adrian Jackson to do.'

'He didn't make an arse of it, did he?'

'Just the opposite; Jade said he was perfect.' Jade was one of Robert's team, the girl Adam Melrose called Si.

'So what are you whining about? You got what you wanted, didn't you?'

'Not quite.' Robert sat back in the big luxury office chair. 'Every time we've warned somebody in the past, they've taken a telling. Usually, we offer them the chance to keep their kneecaps, or their looks. Or keep their sexual organs intact. That last one usually doesn't need to be spelled out. But seeing it was Jean, I didn't want to threaten her son with anything quite so crude. And that was where I went wrong.'

Michael sat forward. 'Tell me what happened.'

'I just got a call from Melrose. He's pished. After he called me all the wankers under the sun, he then told me he'd been to see his mother. Told her what we'd concocted.'

Michael stood up. 'Get t'fuck.'

'Oh, it gets better; he also told her that he was

considering bringing the kids to see her, but now that's off the table.'

'Uh oh. Do you think she'll rip you apart when you get home?'

'No, she'll come here and do it.'

'How do you know?'

Robert drank some more whisky before answering. 'Because no sooner had I got off the phone with ding-a-ling, then his mother phoned. She's on her way over.'

'Well, rather you than me. I'm off.'

'Sit down. I want a buffer. You know I'm no good at this sort of pish. If it was some other bint, I'd have one of my female operatives give her a slap, but this is the woman I live with. Coming to air our dirty laundry in public.'

'So long as you don't expect me to slap her.'

'Nobody is slapping anybody. Look, maybe it *is* better if you piss off somewhere. Tell Greg to get in here.' Greg Sampson, Molloy's head of security.

Michael nodded. 'I have to go and see a man about a dog.'

'Stay away from Adam Melrose. I'll be lucky if Jean is still my girlfriend by tonight.'

Then there was a knock on the door.

TWENTY-ONE

'Look at them,' McIver said from the back seat of the Range Rover as they drove past the electronically-controlled gate at the exit from the underground car park beneath Richard Sullivan's apartment block.

'They're just trying to make a living,' Kim said, easing the big car past the paparazzi. None of them gave her a second glance. McIver had slunk down even though nobody could see in.

'Don't tell me you condone what they do? They're like bloody wolves, baying for blood. Guilty until proven innocent with them.'

'I don't condone men who kill their wives if that's what you mean.'

'Listen, I don't want this to go downhill, you and me. I want you to know that I didn't do anything to hurt my wife. Physically. And to be honest, I don't even think she minded me fooling around. She did the same and we were both happy.'

Kim drove along Ocean Drive, heading towards Newhaven, taking the lower road so she could connect with Trinity.

'Have you ever felt like just running away, Kim?'

'I swear to God, McIver—'

He laughed from the back seat. 'No, no, I don't mean I'm going to do a runner. This isn't a taxi, after all. But I mean, are there ever times when you can't see the light at the end of the tunnel? That even the most exciting days are just simply blah?'

'Not really. I think that life is what you make it.'

'Oh, come on. Aren't there days when being married to Frank gets on your wick? That having the kids screaming and running around makes you want to skip off without telling anybody?'

She thought about the times when Emma could be overpowering but didn't every mother think that way? That the kids not listening was driving her mental? Then she saw where McIver was going with this.

'You trying to paint a picture of what your wife could have done?' she said.

'No, I'm telling you what my wife *did*. There were times when she would take off for the weekend. I knew she was going with other men, of course, but it was the life we led. Sometimes having it away with somebody else keeps a marriage fresh.'

She stopped at a traffic light, braking a little bit too hard. 'How do you know so much about me? About my husband, my kids?'

He didn't flinch. Keeping your reflexes sharp in prison helped you stay intact. He smiled. 'Kim, Richard told me about you and Frank. We chatted over coffee, and I think the chat was meant to be more of a warning. There's nothing nefarious about it.'

She pulled away when the light changed. 'If you think you can get to me through my children, just remember that I am firearms trained and I will blow your fucking head off without even missing a beat.'

'I like that in a woman; toughness.' He saw her looking at him in the mirror and smiled again. 'Look, I'm just trying to give you the story, the one that statements and testimony can't give you. The one thing the police don't have is motive. Sure, we fought at times. Becky had the temper about her, let me tell you. She was spirited. But we didn't hurt each other physically. I honest to God don't know what happened to her.'

'Let me ask you this; do you think she's dead?'

'I don't really know now. Becky wouldn't have left the kids this long. I can tell you this though; if she is dead, I didn't kill her.'

He was looking out of the window as she drove

along Lindsay Road. 'By God, this place has changed so much. Flats where factories used to be.'

'There are more flats over by the water. A fitness centre, hotel, supermarket.'

'Everything changes in the blink of an eye.'

She turned left into Craighall Road and at the top, turned right at the mini roundabout and drove along East Trinity Road.

'You can guide me from here,' she said.

'Go right along. It's on the right. Trinity Road.'

A few minutes later she turned into it.

He told her where to stop. 'That's it right there, Kim. My old house. God, I miss this place.'

McIver was looking out of the window. The sky had cleared and it would have seemed like a summer's day if it wasn't for the chill wind.

They stepped out of the Range Rover and McIver turned to look at the Pentland Hills in the distance.

The house was on the corner with Zetland Place. It was large with a wall on the east side.

'Good memories but some bad ones as well,' he said, almost under his breath.

'I have the keys,' Kim said. 'The letting agency informed the renters that we were coming. They had no choice but to let us in, but don't go raking about.'

They walked up to the door and Kim used the key to let them in.

The house was quiet, but Kim shouted just in case. There was no answer.

'What are you hoping to find here, Kim?' McIver stopped in the hallway, the stairs in front of them.

'Obviously Frank worked on this case six years ago but I didn't. I just want to get a feel for the place. Since this was the last place your wife was seen alive.'

'If she is indeed dead. Even though they think I murdered her, there's never been any body found.'

'Neither has she ever been spotted.'

'Women can make themselves change in a heart-beat. Dye your hair, bit of lippy, short skirt, suddenly Mrs Doubtfire becomes Heidi Klum. I mean, if *you* were to put on—'

'Didn't you take me seriously when I warned you earlier?'

'Of course. I'm just saying. If somebody wants to disappear, they'll disappear, no matter what.'

'Did your wife have money stashed away?'

McIver shrugged. 'If it was stashed away, then I wouldn't have known about it. But she came from money, so in theory, she could have.'

'Who owns this house now?' she said, walking into the living room.

'It went into a trust fund for my kids.'

They went upstairs and Kim went into the bathroom.

'The watch, rings, and other stuff were on the edge of the vanity right there,' McIver said, pointing, in case Kim didn't know what a vanity was.

'And when the forensics crew came back, the items were gone, as was evidenced by the new photos. And nobody was in here except for Lothian and Borders. Is that correct?'

'That's it. The defence pissed all over it and the jury – who I don't consider my peers, by the way – scoffed at the idea. I'm surprised none of them brought their knitting with them.'

'And six years later, Adele Mason, who was once a babysitter for you, is found dead with those items on her.'

'Correct.'

Kim moved out of the bathroom and into one of the bedrooms. 'How did she get them?' she said out loud, more to herself than to McIver. 'What's that over there? A park?'

'Yes, Lomond Park.'

They went into another room and she looked out the window. McIver stood beside her. 'See? There's the door in the wall. That's the side of the house. If the copper was parked out front, he wouldn't see Becky sneak in and enter the house.'

Kim turned to him. 'I want to ask you something; if

you didn't kill your wife and she didn't disappear, then who would want your wife dead?'

McIver looked thoughtful for a moment. 'Somebody who would have motive to want her out of the way. I don't know what the answer is.'

TWENTY-TWO

Miller, Gibb, and Watt drove out to the west side of the city. The afternoon had grown dark again. The day had been like a black-and-white TV that kept fading and needed a slap to stop the picture from going fuzzy.

'Is that where his nibs works?' Watt said from the front passenger seat.

'What are you havering about now?' Gibb said.

'Steffi Walker's boyfriend. Longstone depot. Lothian Buses.' Watt pointed to his left.

'I think it's Central, down in Annandale Street,' Miller said, turning left into Murrayburn Road.

'Rather him than me,' Gibb said. 'I spent some time up in the Wester Hailes station round the corner and we had some wankers to deal with on those buses. I remember one prick took a swing at me one night. I was still in uniform, and the bus was en route to the stop over there. The drunken sod hadn't read the screen and got all stroppy with the driver. So we were called to haul his arse off.'

'And he left with a pair of sore balls,' Watt said. 'Me and Paddy were on the same shift back then, too. I remember that.'

'Let's just hope we don't need to do the same here today,' Miller said, turning right and then left into the crescent with a little grass area in front of it.

They stopped in front of the property they were looking for; an upper level flat in a block of four.

Ben Robertson answered the door wearing jogging pants and a T-shirt. 'I thought you said you were coming round this afternoon?' he said, yawning.

'It is the afternoon,' Watt said, looking disdainfully at the younger man.

'Oh. Okay, you better come in then.' He stepped back to let the detectives in. 'The door on the right,' he instructed, closing the door behind them. They all climbed the stairs to the upper level.

His sister, Cara, was sitting smoking, but she was at least dressed. She looked at them as they came in.

'The Spanish Inquisition, Edinburgh contingent,' she said, by way of a welcome.

'You live here?' Watt said.

'Nope. He lives here. I just come round so we can do our editing.'

'Christ, Cara, these are detectives, not council tax collectors,' Ben said.

Cara shrugged and carried on smoking.

Another two young men entered the room. Marty Williams, the other member of the YouTube film maker crew, and their friend Josh Riley.

'He lives here too,' Cara said without being invited, nodding to Williams.

'There are two bedrooms,' Ben said quickly. 'The third bedroom upstairs is our editing suite. Where Marty and Josh were.'

Williams was also in tracksuit bottoms and a T-shirt. 'Morning, gentlemen,' he said.

'I suppose it's morning somewhere,' Gibb said.

'You said we could view the footage of your trip to the bunker,' Miller said, 'so if you could get it up on a screen, then we won't hold you back any more than is necessary.'

'I have it ready over here,' Ben said, sitting down at a little desk in the corner of the room. 'We do our editing up there, on the iMac, but you can see the results on this laptop just fine.'

He played a video for them, Gibb resisting the urge to put on his reading glasses.

'I film both ways, so we can edit different perspectives in.'

The three detectives watched as Josh ran ahead on the screen.

'How do you know Josh?' Miller said.

'He's an old friend of the family.' He looked at Josh.

Josh smiled and nodded.

'Like we could have used any of that footage with him running about,' Cara said from behind them.

'Christ, is that anyway to talk about somebody with learning difficulties?' Ben said, looking at his sister. Josh stood grinning, not seemingly offended by the remark.

'I wouldn't trust him as far as I could spit him, so next time we go on a shoot, I don't want that bastard coming along.'

'Never mind her,' Ben said to Josh, who stood standing like he hadn't even heard her. Then Josh turned and left the room.

'You should really bite your tongue,' Gibb said to her.

They watched the footage until it stopped with Josh running back out.

'How long in advance did you plan this trip?' Miller asked.

'A couple of weeks. I contacted the guy who's in charge of turning it into a museum, and he asked the owner if it was okay, and then he gave us the go-ahead.

It won't always be there for us to film when it's finished and the public can look around.'

'How many people knew you were going to be there? People that you know?' Gibb asked.

Ben looked at his sister, who just made a face and carried on smoking.

'In our small circle of friends, probably four, if you include Josh. But I can't account for the people who are refurbishing the place.'

'They've been interviewed and cleared. They're decent people, not a rampaging hoard of Vikings,' Gibb said.

'One of them might have talked. Spread it around we were coming.'

'Get a lot of autograph hunters, do you?' Watt said.

'Yeah, he gets groupies bombarding him wherever he goes,' Cara said, nodding to her brother.

'Hey, I do alright. In fact, remember when we did that abandoned psychiatric hospital? A woman contacted me, saying she wanted to have my babies.'

'Probably a former patient,' Marty said, laughing. His hair was ruffled as if he had had a rough night.

'That's just jealousy, mate.'

'If you say so.'

'I do.'

Williams shook his head. 'You boys have any leads yet?'

Gibb looked at him. 'We're following a number of leads, thank you.'

'Oh yeah?' Cara said. 'We should be expecting an arrest imminently, then? Or is that just some more police techno talk?'

'So sceptical for one so young,' Gibb said.

Cara made a face at him and turned away.

'Tell me more about your friend, Josh,' Miller said, sitting down on the arm of a chair.

'What's to tell?' Ben said.

'How well do you know him? How often do you see him? That sort of thing.'

'Didn't you interview him?' Cara said, interrupting.

'If we could just stick to what we asked,' Watt said, disliking the young woman more with each passing second.

Ben held a hand up at his sister. 'It's fine, Cara. Relax.' He looked at Miller. 'Our mother is friends with Josh's mother. Josh lost his father years ago, like we did. I don't know where our mothers met, but somewhere along the line, we met Josh. We knew he was special and our mother asked if we could take him out with us one day. We did. I think it was to the Forth rail bridge?' He looked around for confirmation and Williams nodded.

'That was the first time. He's been on a few trips

with us since. It's no problem taking him along with us. He's challenged, of course, but he's harmless.' He looked at his sister. 'Despite what Cara says.'

'I already told you, if he's on the next trip, I'm not going.'

'Don't be so dramatic.' Ben shook his head.

'Have any of you heard of somebody called *Lord Snooty*?' Miller said.

'Isn't he a politician?' Williams said.

'You're thinking of Screaming Lord Sutch or something,' Cara said.

'Bit before your time, wasn't he?' Watt said.

'So were the Wright Brothers, but I still know about them.'

'Fair enough.'

'Is that a *yes* or a *no* on *Snooty*?' Gibb said, clearly irritated.

'No.'

'No.'

'No.'

The three young people stood looking at the detectives like it was a Mexican standoff.

'What about Adele Mason, the victim?' Gibb said.

'We gave statements,' Cara said to Gibb.

'So did the Yorkshire Ripper.' He glared at Cara.

'No, we didn't,' she replied, stubbing out what was left of her cigarette.

The two men both shook their heads.

'Think about things and give us a call if you remember anything.' Gibb indicated for Miller and Watt to follow him. Miller stood up from the arm of the chair and they trooped out of the room and down the stairs.

Ben followed them and stood by the open door as the detectives walked out onto the path. 'I'm sorry about my sister. She's always been a grumpy boot.'

They walked away and got back in the car.

'Bunch of lying bastards,' Gibb said, lighting up a cigarette like he was in a race. 'And she smoked a ciggie without asking me if I wanted one.'

'I agree,' Miller said. 'They know more than they're letting on.'

Watt nodded. 'That moaning cow routine was meant to make us uncomfortable.'

'It didn't work,' Miller said.

'Of course it didn't,' Watt said. 'Although she gave Paddy a run for his money and nobody's more grumpy than him.'

'Give her her dues, she didn't know who she was up against.'

'Just get the bloody car going,' Gibb said, blowing smoke into the front of the car.

'No further confirmation needed,' Watt said as Miller drove away.

TWENTY-THREE

The rain was getting heavier, thundering on the roof of the car as it entered the cemetery through the gates at the end of Warriston Gardens.

'Same place as the last time, Greg,' Robert Molloy said from the back seat.

'Yes, sir,' Sampson replied as he steered the big Range Rover round to the left. He drove slowly along the track, the puddles splashing off the bodywork of the vehicle.

A hedgerow was on the left, further along from the caretaker's house. Molloy wasn't sure if it actually housed a caretaker, or if it had been sold off. The car stopped at the end of the hedgerow. Sampson looked at Molloy to see if he should drive down into the new part of the cemetery.

'Wait here,' Molloy said, grabbing an umbrella. He

got out, opened the brolly and started walking down the track.

He had waited for Jean to turn up at his office, feeling more nervous than he had felt in a long time. Usually nothing ever worried him because in his mind, every problem had a solution. But with Jean it was different. He had known her for a very long time, and now she was in his life as his girlfriend, he didn't want to lose her.

'Soppy old bastard,' he said out loud as the rain bounced off the umbrella.

Michael would have been aghast at him walking down here on his own. His son went everywhere expecting somebody to jump out at him. He carried a knife, as did his men, along with an array of weapons. But sometimes, Robert just wanted to be on his own.

Jean hadn't turned up at his office. He'd been expecting her like he'd told Michael and decided that after she'd told him to go fuck himself, he would tell her she could live in one of his rental properties. That scenario had been going through his mind while he was waiting for her, but she hadn't shown up.

Now he felt sick. He'd called but there had been no answer. He'd left messages but no reply. He'd wondered where she had gone. He'd called George Stone and the man had confirmed Adam Melrose's story. He'd said that Jean was upset.

Jean's daughter Abi's grave was beyond the small stand of trees. The rain fizzled off them like it was electric. He walked down the track and along a pathway until he came to a break in the trees.

He looked through but couldn't see Jean. He'd been sure this was the one place she would come to.

'You're just a useless old sod, Molloy,' he said and was about to turn back when he saw it. A shoe and a trouser leg sticking out from behind a gravestone. He felt his heart racing for a moment, thinking he should run back to get Sampson, but it looked like a woman's shoe.

He ran, awkwardly with the umbrella up, towards the grave, and his breath left his lungs as he looked down at Jean's soaked body. He saw the hair that was plastered to her head, the rain spattering off her face, but most of all, his eyes were drawn to the blood that was being washed off the cuts on her wrists.

He saw the steak knife lying next to her body. He tried to shout her name, but no words would come out. For the first time in a very long time, Robert Molloy panicked. He fumbled for his mobile phone, taking it out of his pocket but he dropped it.

'Jean!' he finally managed to scream. Then he turned back to face the way he'd come. 'Greg! Greg! Help!' he shouted at the top of his lungs. He knew the man would be sitting with the engine off and the window slightly down so he could hear if the boss needed help.

This was the first time it paid off.

The engine started up and a few seconds later the big car came screaming down the track, almost knocking down a couple of gravestones as he saw Molloy standing waving at him. The umbrella was thrown to one side.

Sampson jumped out, ready to go into combat but Molloy was pointing to the ground.

'It's Jean, Greg! I think she's dead! Fuck me, I think she's dead.' Molloy stood sobbing.

Sampson brushed past the boss without saying a word and knelt down, putting two fingers on Jean's neck.

'She's still alive,' he said, taking his jacket off. He ripped his shirt off and the rain soaked through his T-shirt. He tore the shirt into strips. 'Call treble nine. Get them to meet us at the main road. Hurry, boss!'

Molloy took a deep breath and composed himself, knowing Jean was counting on them. He picked up his phone and made the call for the ambulance. Sampson made the strips from his shirt into bandages, tying them tightly around Jean's wrists to stop the bleeding. He then sat her up and put his jacket round her. Her head flopped backwards as he started towards the car.

Molloy picked up the knife and the umbrella, closing it.

'Boss, get the back door open.'

Molloy rushed forward and opened the door. Sampson put Jean in the seat, keeping her upright.

'Get round the other side and sit in beside her, boss. Keep pressure on the wounds and her arms raised.'

Molloy rushed round and got in. He grabbed a hold of Jean, pulling her close to him as Sampson closed the door and got in behind the wheel. He drove round the gravestones like this was an everyday occurrence, dodging the stones like he was an expert rally driver and he was back out onto the track and racing for the exit. He slowed and got round the final obstacle, flooring it out of the exit.

Warriston Gardens was a long, straight road, leading from the cemetery to the main road, Inverleith Row. He started to slow at the rugby ground just as the ambulance came round the corner. Sampson flashed the lights and had his hand out the window.

The big car stopped next to the ambulance and the paramedics took over. The police hadn't been called. Molloy had said a woman had collapsed in the cemetery. He hadn't mentioned anything about her wrists being cut. He'd said he thought she was having a heart attack, guaranteeing a rapid response without the awkward questions the police would have. Those would come later.

It didn't take the medics long to get Jean strapped onto a stretcher and into the back of the ambulance.

She was alive, but Molloy had seen a lot of blood.

'Greg, follow the ambulance. Right behind it, son.'

They got back in and the two vehicles hit the main road.

Molloy called his son. Told him what was going on.

'Do what you do best. I'll call you later.'

Adam Melrose sat on his expensive leather couch with another glass of wine and watched some stupid TV show. He didn't watch much TV nowadays, sticking to Netflix if he wanted to binge. It kept his girlfriend happy, although he liked to think that he wasn't the reason she stuck around.

She was coming round later on. He knew he shouldn't be drinking so much but he was so pissed off at his mother that the anger was rising to the surface again.

Not mother but *step*-mother, he reminded himself. Fucking Jean. Drove his father away and now she was driving him away too. Well, fuck her. He'd teach the old bag a lesson.

He got up from the couch to pour some more wine but stopped to admire the view first. This was a small, exclusive, apartment building on Ravelston Terrace. No riff-raff here, that was for sure. Unlike the hovel his girlfriend's brother lived in.

The doorbell rang.

He looked at his watch. A Rolex Submariner. Not one of those flashy *come and rob me* numbers, but a watch with elegance.

He smiled. This would be her now. She was early, but he was hardly going to tell her that.

He strode through to the front door and opened it wide. 'Hi, honey.'

Then he looked at the two police officers standing there.

'Can we come in, Mr Melrose? We need a word.'

'Of course. What's it about?' He stood to one side and then another figure stepped into view. Michael Molloy. Then he knew what it was about. But before he could put up a fight, the two fake uniforms were all over him.

TWENTY-FOUR

'It's called, *turning a blind eye*,' Kim said, as Frank Miller put two mugs of coffee down on the table.

'It's called *unethical* by Professional Standards.'

Jack Miller, his father, was sitting on the window sill as if Gus McIver would make a break for it that way instead of trying the front door. They were in Frank and Kim's apartment. Jack lived along the hallway after moving in with his girlfriend.

'Let me put this into perspective,' Jack said. 'Kim's mother is the PF, and the Crown Office sanctioned McIver's release.' He looked over at McIver who was sitting on the settee smiling at everybody. 'Her father, Neil McGovern, is in charge of the government witness protection, Scottish Office, and has asked me to babysit him for a little while.

'Look on this as a staging post. We're gathered here,

until McGovern's car comes to pick us up, then we're going down to see him in his office. There's nothing underhand going on, and if Standards thinks there is, let them take it up with McGovern. He'll chew them a new arsehole.'

'I don't think that's going to be a problem, Jack,' Kim said.

'Me neither,' McIver said. 'Nice flat by the way. How much do these run for nowadays?'

'Not as much as your house in Trinity,' Kim replied.

'I'm the one who's going to get it in the neck,' Frank complained. 'You could have taken him to the station.'

Jack turned and pulled the curtain back a bit. 'There are more of those paparazzi up there. Even if you drove down to the rear car park, they'd see you.' His phone buzzed in his pocket and he took it out. Answered, then hung up.

'Come on then, McIver, our chariot awaits. And let me reiterate, if you try and run, the last thing you'll have to worry about is photographers.'

'I'm sensing this threat of bodily harm thing runs in the family.' McIver stood up. At six five, Jack towered over the smaller professor. 'I think I could outrun you, but not beat you in a fist fight, and I'm not really into running.'

'Just hold that thought.' Jack looked at Kim.

'Samantha's having a blast with the girls, so don't worry about a thing. Just enjoy the time off.'

'Thanks, Jack.'

Samantha Willis was an American crime writer and Jack's live-in girlfriend.

'Take it easy, Dad. Give me a call later,' Frank said.

'Will do.'

Jack and McIver left and went downstairs to the waiting car.

Five minutes later, they were pulling into the underground car park at the back of the Scottish Parliament building on Holyrood Road and then they were taken to McGovern's office.

'Ah, Mr McIver, man of the hour!' Neil McGovern said as the two of them came in.

'McIver, this is Mr McGovern.'

'It's Professor McIver, actually, but no biggie.' He smiled when he shook hands with McGovern.

'My mistake. Professor. Please, sit down.'

They both took seats as McGovern poured them a coffee. 'You might wonder why you're here,' he said sitting down.

'Don't you have all freed prisoners here?' McIver said.

'First of all, *professor*, you are not a free man. You're out on license because doubt has been thrown on your conviction. My wife, Norma Banks, is the PF who orchestrated your release at short notice, which I was sceptical about. Usually, when we're protecting somebody, a lot of thought has gone into it, but since you're not in witness protection, it is not in my remit to offer protection.

'However, since my daughter, Kim, will be doing a parallel investigation for the Crown Office, she will be touching base with you. Therefore, you will attend any meeting requested by my daughter. In other words, you will not go for a shit without me knowing about it. Do you understand me?' Gone was the smile and the hint of bonhomie, to be replaced by a smile that a shark would be proud of.

'Yes.'

'Good. Jack will be around as well since my daughter is busy with her own children in the evenings and weekends. If you need anything out of business hours, give him a call. He's on my payroll, so he will be reporting to me. You will not leave Richard Sullivan's flat without permission. If he and his wife are not there, either Jack or Kim will be. I do hope this is sinking in?'

'Fine. I won't talk about any of this. I've had my fill of being in prison. I have no desire to go back.'

'Good. Now that we're on the same page, I want you to speak freely. Tell me who you think killed your wife. And why.'

TWENTY-FIVE

Robert Molloy was sitting outside the ward where Jean Melrose was being cared for. Two more of his men had been summoned and they had brought a change of clothes for Sampson who was sitting next to his boss when the doctor came out of Jean's room. Both men stood up.

'How is she, doc?' Molloy asked. Thoughts of his son, Sean, dying in here ran through his mind.

'She's going to be fine. Thanks to you. Her heart stopped twice because of the blood loss but we got her back.'

'She would have died in that cemetery, wouldn't she?'

'Yes. In all probability, she would have bled out. You got to her in time. You saved her life by going to the cemetery.'

'Can I see her?'

'She's sedated right now, so she won't know you're there. You can see her, certainly, but you won't be able to speak to her until tomorrow.' He smiled at Molloy. 'Good job.'

He walked away and Molloy turned to Sampson. 'You saved her life, you know that?'

'You did, boss. You guessed she was there.'

'I know, but when I saw her, I panicked. I don't panic easily, but I did then. Christ, you took over like it was something you did every day. You knew what to do. I don't know what would have happened if you hadn't been with me. Wait, I do know; Jean would have died. I owe you big time, son. Starting with a big pay rise.'

'There's no need, boss.'

'Like hell, there isn't. Anything you need, you ask me. From now on, you're family.' He patted Sampson on the arm. 'Now, give me a minute while I go in and see the woman I love. The future Mrs Molloy, if she'll have me.'

'I'll be right here, boss.'

Molloy went into the room and saw Jean lying in the bed, attached to a monitor and a drip. She looked so peaceful and quiet that he thought she was dead at first, then he gave himself a mental kick up the arse.

He walked over to her bed and sat down on the chair beside her. He took one of her hands in his.

'Jean, if you can hear me, please know that I love you and I'll do anything I can to make sure you're happy again. I know what you did was my fault. I'm sorry. It won't happen again. I will do everything in my power to make you happy.'

He looked at her face and felt a love for her that he hadn't felt since his first wife.

Molloy let her hand go and stood up quietly. 'I have to go now, my love, but I will be back tomorrow. I love you, Jean.'

He left the room. 'Come on, son, take me to the club on George Street. I have an appointment with somebody.'

The club that Molloy owned was a former bank with a grandiose façade. It was now a very successful bar with a nightclub on the lower level.

Everything had been intact when the bank sold the building. Including the vaults down in the basement.

Robert Molloy's footsteps echoed off the tunnel walls as he made his way along to the vaults, his men behind him.

His son, Michael, was waiting for him in one of the

large rooms. Sitting tied to a chair in the middle of the room was Adam Melrose.

'What the fuck is going on here, Molloy?' Melrose said.

Robert walked right up to Melrose and back-handed him across the face.

'Don't you ever fucking talk to me like that again, you jumped-up little prick!' He grabbed Melrose by the hair. 'Do you know where I've just been?'

'Let me guess? One of your massage parlours.'

Robert held his hand out towards Michael who was standing behind Melrose. Michael handed the gun over. Robert rammed the Glock against Melrose's forehead and only then did Melrose start taking him seriously.

'Do you know what you did? Do you know what you're fucking responsible for?' Molloy was screaming at the other man.

'I didn't do anything!' His face twisted into a snarl.

'Are you trying to take the fucking piss out of me?'

'Christ, all this for yelling at Jean. It's a bit extreme, even for you Molloy.'

Robert's head was starting to spin a bit and he was sweating.

'You listen to me, you little fucking freak show; you should have taken a warning with the laptop, but oh no, that wasn't good enough for you, so now I'm going to tell you something and you'd better listen;

'I love your mother. And when she gets upset, I get upset. This afternoon she tried to take her own life in Warriston cemetery. Luckily, I found her in time and one of my men saved her life. If she had died, I would have cut you into a thousand little pieces with a fucking chainsaw.'

Robert's breath was coming fast now.

Michael looked at his father. 'Give me the gun, Dad, and I'll blow the bastard away now. I'll take his kneecaps off first.'

Robert looked at him. No, Michael, this is a job I have to do.'

Melrose looked panicked now. 'Please, you don't have to do this.'

'Shut the fuck up!' Robert pressed the gun harder against Melrose's forehead. 'This is how it is going to go from now on; you will apologise to your mother for the grief you caused her. You will bring her grandchildren round for a visit. You will smile all the while you're doing it. If not, I will have some nasty bastard take your knackers off with a pair of rusty garden shears, just before we start to break your fucking bones. You will die in a lot of pain. If you want to call my bluff, just you try and keep those bairns away from her. Do I make myself clear?'

'Yes.' Melrose wasn't looking so sure of himself now.

'And if you ever tell your mother we had this conversation, same deal. You understand?'

'Yes.'

Robert Molloy stood back and pistol-whipped Melrose across the face. 'That's for calling me a wanker on the phone.' He looked at Michael. 'Get the fucker cleaned up. I want him to take a bunch of flowers in to his mother. Make sure somebody drives him there tomorrow. If he's not waiting for my men, put out a hit on him.'

'I'll be there.' Blood was coming out of his mouth now.

'See how easy it was to get into your apartment? I can have it made to look like anybody; utility workers, anybody. You will never see it coming.'

He walked away with Michael and stood outside in the corridor.

'I'm going home. I feel fucked.'

'Do that, Dad.'

'I meant what I said; if he fucks me around, waste him. Make the cunt feel pain first.'

'My pleasure.'

'Oh, and by the way; Greg Sampson saved Jean's life. I want that boy treated with utmost respect from now on. And he's getting a big pay rise. See that it happens.'

'You got it.'

Robert walked away along the corridor with his men.

TWENTY-SIX

'Frank, can we take Annie to the park this weekend? I think she wants to go on the swings,' Emma said to Miller. They were in the kitchen having breakfast.

'Of course we can, honey. We can take a bag of bread to feed the ducks.'

'Yay. I can help push Annie in her pram.' Miller's stepdaughter smiled as she put her dish on the counter. Kim came in, holding the baby.

'We're going to the park at the weekend, Mum!' Emma shouted.

'That's great. As long as it doesn't pour down with rain.'

'Why? Ducks like the water. Tell her, Frank.' She smiled as she left the kitchen.

'I swear that girl is going to be a handful when it comes time for dating,' Kim said.

'Thankfully, she'll have her dad and me to sort out any young man who isn't suitable,' Miller said as his wife passed Annie over.

'I don't envy her future husband; an SAS soldier and a detective to deal with. Although by that time, Eric might have left the army.'

'Still doesn't make him any less hard,' Miller said, bouncing the baby up and down on his knee.

'Unless you want regurgitated milk all over your clean shirt and trousers, I'd stop doing that.'

'Oops.' He made faces at his daughter instead. 'You know, I wish you didn't have to babysit McIver.'

'Why?' Kim asked as she poured herself a coffee.

Miller shrugged. 'I don't know. It's just a feeling I get about him.'

'Jesus, Miller, you're not getting jealous, are you?'

'What? No, of course not. I just can't get a handle on him.'

'You don't think he's innocent?'

'It's not that, Kim. I just think he's... smarmy.'

'He is a bit. But let me put this to you; if he's guilty, or I should say, the Crown Office believe he's still guilty, he'll be taken back to Saughton.'

'We're still delving into Adele Mason's background. The biggest mystery is how she got that jewellery on her.'

'The killer obviously didn't know she had that stuff

on her. That's my guess. Since it was in that pocket in her jacket. I mean, Josh only saw it because the material had rotted away.'

'We don't think it was a robbery, although we can't be absolutely certain. I mean, a robber doesn't kill someone then dump the body. This was a murder, pure and simple.'

Kim sat opposite him and Annie smiled at her. 'And isn't the old adage that most murder victims know their killer?'

'It's a fact.'

'Who would want Adele dead? And why?'

'You haven't met some of the weirdos she hung out with. Studenty types,' Miller said.

'Studenty isn't a word. Don't be saying things like that around Annie. I don't want her to pick up your bad habits.'

'Don't worry, she'll still have her father's intelligence.' He looked across at Kim staring at him. He laughed. 'And her mother's, of course.'

Kim drank some more coffee and smiled back. 'The babysitter will be here shortly. And I have to go and see McIver. Babysit *him*.'

'I thought my dad was doing that? Jack wouldn't take any guff off him.'

'*I* won't take any guff off him! Miller.'

'I meant Jack would slap him around if need be.'

'I work for the Crown Office. I'll pretend I didn't hear that.' She stood up from the table.

'I meant in self-defence.'

'Sure you did.' She finished her coffee and put her mug and her daughter's cereal bowl in the dishwasher. 'I'll see you tonight at dinner. Love you. Despite your cheek.'

'Love you too. And you too, little lady.' He kissed Annie as he passed her back to her mother. Then he made a call to Steffi Walker.

'While I remember, I'd like you to do something for me.'

'*Sure, boss.*'

He told her what he wanted before leaving the flat.

Robert Molloy walked along to Jean's room and waited outside in the corridor while one of his men went to find a doctor. The man in the white coat came along a few minutes later.

'How is she, doc?

'Mr Molloy, I'm happy to say that Mrs Melrose is awake and in much better spirits.'

Molloy took a deep breath and let it out slowly, to quell the anger rising up inside. 'That's good news, but let me ask you; what's the long-term situation? Where do we go from here?'

'I'm sorry, but she's going to be in here for a few days. The wounds will heal, but before we can release her, she has to speak with a psychologist. Just to make sure she's heading in the right direction. We want her well before she goes home, which I'm sure you can understand.'

'Yes, yes, I do. Can I speak to her now?'

'Yes, go ahead. Her son is with her now. If you need any more information, please don't hesitate to ask, or give me a call.' He shook hands with Molloy.

Greg Sampson was standing behind Molloy, holding a bunch of flowers. 'Thanks, pal. Go and get a coffee. Leave one of the others outside in case I need somebody slapped.'

'Yes, sir.'

Molloy knocked and opened the door, smiling. Adam Melrose was sitting in a chair and scooted it back when Molloy entered. Jean smiled at him.

'Mr Molloy, good to see you again.' He stood up. 'Please, have this chair.'

'That's a nasty cut on your face there, son. What happened?'

Melrose looked at him uncertainly for a moment. 'I was drunk. I tripped and fell down some stairs. No big deal.'

'You should take care of yourself. Accidents can happen anytime.'

Melrose nodded and looked down at his mother. 'I'll be back in tonight again, Mum. If that's okay with Mr Molloy.'

'Of course it is, son. You can come and see your mum anytime.'

Melrose kissed his mother and left. Molloy stepped forward with the flowers. 'I didn't get too big a bunch, not because I'm cheap, but because I wasn't sure how big the vases were.'

He looked round to watch Melrose leave. Greg Sampson looked at his boss and gave a little smile before quietly closing the door behind him, leaving them alone.

'Oh, God, Robert, I am so sorry,' Jean said. She started crying. Molloy put the flowers down on the chair and bent down to hug her.

'You've nothing to be sorry about.'

He held her for a few minutes while she cried some more. He didn't want her to see his own tears. Then he let go, moved the flowers to another chair and sat down next to her bed.

'They told me you saved me. How did you know where I would be?'

'It was a hunch. But Greg saved your life. He took over while I stood like a headless chicken. He went to work and stopped the blood flow. Christ, Jean, I can't even imagine if I'd got there fifteen minutes later.'

'My head was spinning. I couldn't think straight. At that moment in time, I just wanted to be with my little girl. My son didn't want to know me, I wasn't going to see my grandchildren again. I knew you were there, my love, but that's the part I couldn't think straight about. If I had, then I'd have known I would be leaving behind the man who loves me. I'm so sorry. I promise you I will never do anything like that again.'

'I'm glad to hear that. I couldn't do without you in my life.' He squeezed her hand. 'Did you get things sorted with Adam?'

'Yes. He told me he made up that story about you taking his laptop. He was just trying to hurt me. I should have known better. But he was so apologetic and promised me I could see my little grandchildren whenever I want. He's a changed man, Robert.'

I'll bet he is. 'All's well that ends well, as the saying goes.'

They chatted for a while then Robert stood up. 'They want you to chat to somebody, then they're going to let you go home.'

'I can't wait to come home.'

'It won't be long, but I'll come and see you every day until then.'

He walked out of the room and saw a familiar face outside.

'I'd like to go and see her,' Andy Watt said.

Molloy looked at him for a second. 'Go ahead.' He nodded for his men to step aside and Watt knocked and entered.

'Hello, Jean.'

She was silent for a moment, as if she was seeing a ghost. 'Come in, Andy.'

He entered and closed the door behind him. 'I just wanted to see how you were doing. I heard, obviously.'

'Sit down. I don't want you to feel awkward.'

Watt shook his head. 'I'll stand. I just want you to know I'm not here looking for forgiveness. What I did was wrong. But it doesn't mean I didn't care about you.'

'Well, you don't have to worry about it. I didn't do what I did because of what happened between us.'

'I didn't think it was that. You're too strong a woman for that.'

'Not strong enough.'

Watt looked at his shoes for a moment before looking up. 'Anyway, I just wanted to say, I hope you're happy with Molloy. I really mean that.'

'Thank you.'

'I should be going. We're working on a case.'

'Okay. Thank you for coming by, Andy.'

'I passed Adam in the corridor. What happened to his face?'

'I think Robert had somebody hit him, although Robert would never admit that. Adam overstepped the mark and he wasn't going to bring the girls round again.'

'Ooh. And he had the balls to tell you that, knowing who you're living with?'

'I don't think he knew the gravity of the situation. He does now though. And now I get to see the girls whenever I want to.'

'All's well that ends well,' Watt said as he opened the door.

'Funny, Robert said that too.'

Outside, Adam Melrose got in the waiting car.

'How is she?' the driver asked.

'Never mind that. I managed to look like the concerned son.'

'They did do a number on you.'

'That fucking Molloy was there. Surrounded by people, so I couldn't punch him in the face.'

'Look what happened the last time you tried to get the better of him.'

Melrose made a face. 'That won't happen again.'

'Are you going to work?'

'Does it look like I'm going to work? How would I explain my face looking like this? I told them I have a family emergency, which is true. I left out the fact my face looks like a horse kicked it.'

'So what now?'

'I just have to keep that old bitch happy and Molloy will leave me alone. It's a small price to pay.'

'There is another way.'

Melrose raised his eyebrows as the driver started the car and drove away. 'Tell me more.'

TWENTY-SEVEN

'Come on, Kim,' Gus McIver said. 'You could be by my side every step of the way.'

'You know I can't do that.'

'Can't or won't?' He was standing at Richard Sullivan's back door that led onto the small balcony, where people could sit and gaze out over the sea to Fife in the summer time.

'Don't be pedantic.'

'Oh, come on. Please? I'm literally begging you now, Kim. I will just look from afar. She won't even recognise me, considering she hasn't seen me in six years.'

Richard Sullivan sat at the dining table drinking a coffee. 'What harm would it do, Kim?'

'If he buggers off, then my career is over.' She

looked back at McIver. 'And then your life would be over.'

'Jeez, you should talk to somebody about those anger issues you have.'

'Cut it out, Gus,' Sullivan said.

'Okay, I'm sorry. All I want to do is see my little girl come out of school. You're a mother, Kim. How would you feel if somebody wouldn't let you see your kids?'

Kim sat down beside Sullivan and looked at him. 'If I go along, you're coming with me, since you're on his side about this.'

'Fine. I'll be there,' Sullivan replied.

She looked at McIver. 'I swear, if you're trying it on, I will rip you a new one.'

McIver smiled and held out his hands. 'Thank you. I promise I won't do anything stupid.'

'You heard him,' she said to Sullivan. 'But be warned; if this is some plot cooked up by the two of you, you will regret ever setting eyes on me.'

'Living with Frank has obviously rubbed off,' Sullivan said.

'Do you talk to Tai like that?'

'I wouldn't dare.'

'There's a fine line here, Richard. Don't cross it.'

'Yeah, Dickie. Show the girl some respect.'

'Shut up and get ready to leave. This is your one window of opportunity.'

Lord Snooty listened to the voice on the other end of the phone and looked at Princess. 'It's a go. The old boy is in one of his pubs and the other two are in George Street.'

'Let's do it, then, before somebody comes along and starts asking questions.'

They got out of the car in the underground car park and took the elevator up to the top floor.

They walked along the carpeted hallway until they were approaching the flat they wanted. They were wearing woollen hats which they pulled down into balaclavas. This was going to be more about speed, not so much about stealth.

Snooty took the iron bar from his backpack and forced the door open.

'Three minutes,' he said, putting the timer on his phone.

Princess nodded as she closed the door behind her. It wouldn't close all the way but that didn't matter. They each took a room and went through it methodically. They found watches and other valuables as they tossed the place.

In one of the wardrobes, they found a cash box, and under some T-shirts, a laptop. It was an HP, one of the latest Spectre models. Snooty put it in his backpack along with the other stuff.

His phone alarm buzzed from the living room.

'Let's go,' he said.

'We could always stay a bit longer and mess up their bed,' Princess said with a small laugh.

'Let's go,' he repeated, and she pouted.

They left the apartment and went down to the car, taking the balaclavas off before they left the lift.

Inside the car, Snooty opened the backpack and took out the laptop and fired it up.

'That's a nice computer,' Princess said. 'I'm after a new one. Can I keep that?'

'No. This one is all mine.'

He packed the stuff away and drove off.

TWENTY-EIGHT

Kim had parked the Range Rover in Forrester Park Avenue, just off the main road, Broomhouse Road. They walked towards the pedestrian bridge that spanned the road for the school kids to get across safely to the bus stop.

'I won't forget this, Kim,' McIver said.

'Just don't make me shoot you.' She said it with a smile that had no humour.

'Just don't run,' Sullivan said, shrugging into his overcoat. 'You know how I hate running.'

'I'm not running, I'm not doing anything to make you think I'm guilty.' He turned from them and looked across the road at the hoard of school kids coming out, some in uniform, others not. The uniforms were coming from St Augustine's, while the others were from Forrester.

'Will she have a uniform on?' Sullivan asked.

'Yes. Although it's going to be hard spotting her.' There was a sea of dark blue uniforms coming out of the gate, half of them heading up the steps to cross the bridge, while the other half were walking towards the bus stop further up.

'There are school buses that wait on the other side, at South Gyle,' McIver said, 'but I think that's for kids that live further away. Or maybe it's to keep the kids off the public buses. I'm not sure.'

'Do you think she would get on the school bus?'

'I'm not sure. I thought she would be picked up by Dee, to be honest. They live along the far end of South Gyle, but I don't think she would want my daughter walking along there on her own. Dee is over-protective.'

'Why wouldn't she park on the other side of the school, on the South Gyle end?' Sullivan asked.

'And park where? South Gyle is the overflow car park for the people who work in the industrial estate. They don't give a shit how they mess up the parking over there. So if Dee was coming, it's easier to park over here.'

Then he saw her. 'Jesus, there she is. She looks older of course, but I would know my little girl anywhere. My little Tara.'

'Which one? Tell me, don't point,' Kim said.

He described her and after a few tries, Kim and Sullivan picked out the girl he was talking about.

Tara was walking with a group of friends, up and over on the pedestrian bridge. She stopped at the top, took out her mobile phone and made a call.

'Kids nowadays,' McIver said. 'They're never off their phones.'

After a couple of minutes, Tara hung up and carried on down the ramp, which then split into a stepped ramp and stairs in the opposite direction. She went down the steps.

'Can we follow her just a little bit?'

'Sorry, Gus, I can't let you do that,' Kim said.

'Fair enough.' He watched her walk down the pavement towards the Co-op Funeral Directors' building on the same side.

Tara turned around to look at them, just as they heard the sound of a siren coming towards them from the Corstorphine end. They couldn't see it as the road rose up in a hump to go over the Fife railway line.

A car pulled up and stopped in the side road next to the funeral directors.

'Who's that driving the car?' McIver said, almost to himself. It was a young man.

'Does she have a boyfriend?' Kim asked.

'She's fourteen. Of course not.'

'Some girls are mothers at that age.'

The man got out and waved to Tara. Kim took out her phone and zoomed in on the man just as the police car screeched into the side of the road and the two officers jumped out and ran over to them.

Tara turned and looked at them one more time before she reached the car.

'Hold up there!' Kim shouted at the uniforms as they reached them. 'I work with the PF's office.'

'Is that right? We've had a call about a bunch of perverts looking at the kids,' the older one said.

Kim took her ID out and showed it to him. 'I'm here on official business.'

'You got ID?' he said to McIver.

'I'm vouching for him, officer.'

'I still need to see ID.'

Sullivan took his out. 'I'm his lawyer. This lady works for the Crown Office. Your career path is now at a crossroads, son. You can accept the fact that we're here on business and this was a mistake, or by morning, you'll be working at the Police Scotland, Outer Hebrides office.'

The older officer looked at the younger one. 'Yes, sir. My apologies, but we got a treble nine call. We can't take any chances.'

'I agree. But now that we've got this sorted, please don't let us keep you.'

They got back in their car and drove away.

'Did you see where the car went?' Kim said.

'Up towards the roundabout.'

'Shit. Tara obviously saw us and called the police.'

'Do you think she recognised me?'

'Your face *has* been on the news, my friend,' Sullivan said.

'I thought it would be so busy, she wouldn't see me.'

'Kids are smart. It's us old fogies who are dumb,' Sullivan said.

'Speak for yourself,' McIver mumbled as he walked away.

TWENTY-NINE

'Far be it for me to tell you how to behave in your own flat, Rita, but I must say that running a wee Hoover over the place now and again wouldn't do any harm,' Adrian Jackson said as he surveyed the living room.

'Somehow, I don't think a feather duster could cope with this mess,' she replied.

'It's all fun and games until somebody gets an eye out. What say you, Brian?'

Jackson's nephew stood gawping at the mess. 'I think we've been turned over.'

'Give the boy a custard cream. First prize, Brian. But can you tell off-hand what's been taken?'

'Not the TV.'

'I can fucking see that. It's still on the wall. How about something that isn't so obvious?' Then he stopped and stared for a moment. 'Go and get the laptop I gave you for safekeeping.'

Brian walked through to the bedroom and came back a moment later. 'It's gone.'

'What do you mean, it's gone?' Rita said.

'I don't think that needs any more explaining, Rita, love,' Jackson said. 'Those bastards stole it.' He looked back at Brian. 'I am going to pour myself a drink and you will go round here and see what else is missing. Hurry up now.'

He walked over to the cabinet where Rita and Brian kept their drinks and poured himself a hefty measure.

'You have covert security cameras in here,' Jackson said when Brian came back in the room.

'I didn't know that.' The young man stood staring at his uncle like he was having him on. 'I don't like the idea of that at all. What if somebody hacked into it and saw me walking about in my skids?'

'After they'd stopped puking, they'd blind themselves.'

'I'm offended by that remark.'

'I don't think you would have to worry that somebody had watched you walking about half naked and mistook you for David Beckham.'

'Where are they?'

'One's in that wall clock. There's another in the

smoke alarm on your hallway ceiling. So let me log in to the account and bring up the footage.'

'How can you do that with the laptop gone?' Brian said.

'I swear to God. First of all, that wasn't my laptop. The clue was when I used the word *safekeeping*. And secondly, the MacBook Pro is still sitting on the desk.'

'Oh yeah. I wonder why they didn't take that?'

'Because they knew what they were looking for. Rita, be a love and get the MacBook on.'

Rita walked over and lifted the lid on the silver machine and it sprang into life.

Jackson shook his head and sat down at the small desk. Brought up Firefox and typed in an address. When he was on the company's website, he logged in and accessed the videos.

'Just before I hit play, you haven't been chasing Rita about the apartment with no clothes on, have you?'

'I have a healthy respect for Rita, I'll have you know.'

'Yes or no?'

'Once. But that was ages ago.'

'Dirty wee bastard,' Jackson mumbled, and watched the videos from earlier in the day. It showed two figures coming in, wearing balaclavas. They then continued to ransack the apartment but completely ignored the MacBook Pro.

One of them brought the laptop out from the bedroom and held it up like a prize. They put it in a bag along with other stuff and left after trashing the place a bit, like it was an afterthought.

'Bastards. They knew what they were after.' He closed the lid on the laptop after logging out and stood up. 'Did you notice anything about them?'

'One was a woman,' Rita said without hesitation.

'Correct. And I'm having a guess who the other one was.' He stood up. 'Right, get this place cleaned up as best you can. Anything that was broken, I'll have taken care of. I have to go and see a man about a dog.'

THIRTY

'What's this all about, inspector?' Dee Raeburn said. She looked up from the table in the interview room as Paddy Gibb walked in.

Gibb shut the door and sat down next to Miller. He was holding a folder and put it down in front of him.

'We just have a few follow-up questions, Mrs Raeburn,' Miller said.

Gibb opened the folder and looked at a sheet in front of him. 'How good would you say your relationship was with your sister, Becky McIver?'

'I don't understand. What's this all about?'

'Just answer the question.' Gibb looked across the table at her.

'Our relationship was fine. We argued sometimes, but we loved each other.'

'What did you argue about?'

'Her lifestyle, mainly. She and that creep were messing about with other people. It wasn't normal. I told her that but she wouldn't listen, said I was always poking my nose in.'

'I suppose you lucked out when she disappeared,' Gibb said. 'You got to keep her children. Now you can shape them whatever way you want to.'

'What are you trying to say?'

'In Scotland, as in other places, a person can be declared dead after seven years,' Miller said. 'Next year, it will be seven years since your sister went missing, so she can be declared dead, and then the insurance company will have to pay out on her death. Can you tell us for the record who the beneficiary is on her life insurance?'

Dee hesitated for a moment. 'Me.'

'A bit louder for the tape,' Gibb said.

'Me! Okay? I'm the beneficiary, but only because her lousy husband couldn't be trusted to spend the money on the kids. It was her idea, anyway.'

'We only have your word for that,' Miller said.

'I really don't care. She asked me to do it, so I could look after the kids if anything should happen to her.'

'Do you have any kids yourself, Mrs Raeburn?'

'No. We didn't want any. Well, my husband didn't and I went along with it. I did really though. I told him that one day, and he said he would think about it, but he was diagnosed with cancer and he was dead six months later.'

'And now you have a ready-made family.'

'What is it you're trying to get at?' Dee leaned on the table.

'With your sister dead, she would be out of the way. And wouldn't it be great if you could get her husband out of the picture as well? You'd have the kids you always wanted. But kids are expensive. Yes, you would get help from the state but there was a big payday waiting for you. Just sit tight for seven years and you would be on easy street.'

Dee leaned back. 'You know, I pity you both. Having a job where you not only deal with the dregs of life but where you have to sit and make stories up about decent, law-abiding citizens until you come up with some sordid tale. You know my father was loaded. That's why Becky had the house in Trinity. I had a big house in Murrayfield, but after my husband died, I couldn't stay there, with the memories. So I downsized and bought a smaller house in South Gyle.'

Gibb took out a photo that had been blown up from Kim's phone. 'You recognise that man?'

Dee looked at it. 'Of course I do. That's Josh, my friend's son. Why? Where did you take that?'

'He picked up Tara from school,' Miller said.

'I know. He does it every day. He's good at helping me out that way. He does a lot for me.'

'Did you know he was the one who found Adele?' Miller said.

'What? I thought it was Ben?'

'No, it was Josh. He ran ahead of the others when they were filming. We watched the video they shot that day.'

'Really? He didn't say. And the papers just said it was a group of friends who were in there.'

'It was Josh.'

'You know, Josh gets slagged off by that Cara girl. Ben's sister. She's so high and mighty. Thinks she's all that. Butter would melt. She's just another whore, same as Adele was.'

'Okay. Tell us more about her,' Gibb said.

'She's just a spoilt lassie. Her mother and I have known each other for years. Becky always thought she was a little tramp, too. She caught Gus canoodling with her on the couch one night.'

'How old was she?' Miller asked.

'Back then? About twenty-two, twenty-three, something like that. God knows what that girl saw in Gus, but Becky could hardly complain, could she? This was the lifestyle that they had chosen. But Becky just took a dislike to Cara.'

They chatted to her for another ten minutes before ending the interview.

Outside in the corridor, Gibb stretched and yawned. 'I knew there was something about that Cara girl. What the hell did those students see in McIver?'

'It's not all about looks. He had a well-paid job. It's how he talked with women. He knows how to charm them, I'm sure.'

'Well, I'm going home to charm Maggie. I'm going to cook her dinner. See you tomorrow.' He walked away down the corridor with the folder in his hand.

Then the sergeant from the robbery squad came walking along towards him. Sergeant Hooligan.

'Sir, I thought you would want a copy of this sheet. I was going to leave it on your desk. It's the results from the prints on the jewellery that Adele Mason had on her. Nothing jumps out.'

'Thanks, sergeant.'

The robbery cop walked away then he stopped and turned towards Miller again.

'Sir? You were on the rehabilitation team when Adrian Jackson returned to Edinburgh, weren't you?'

'Yes, I was. Why?'

'I just thought you might want to know that his nephew's flat was tanned this afternoon. The place up at Lauriston.'

'Oh really? Thanks for telling me.'

They set off in opposite directions again.

Something was nagging away in the back of his mind. Something he couldn't put his finger on.

He started walking away, figuring it would come to him in its own good time.

THIRTY-ONE

'When's the next time we're going on a job?' Princess asked.

'Why?' Lord Snooty said.

'I enjoy breaking into people's houses.'

'Christ, haven't you ever thought about getting a job as well? People might wonder where you get your money.'

'Let them wonder. I don't care about anybody but you. But I want us to plan something else.'

'We will. Me and the boys have been talking about it. We'll get the ball rolling again soon. They'll be going out next week, and they'll pick up something.'

'Oh, so I don't get involved once again.'

'We were just planning. You know they're integral to our plans. They get the easy job. We do the hard work. We take the risks.'

'I suppose you're right.'

'I know I'm right.'

She put her arm around his shoulders. 'Why don't we have a quiet night in?'

'As much as I'd love to, we have a job to do.'

'I thought you said we didn't have anything planned?' Princess said.

'This is different. It's a job just for you and me.'

'How's it going with McIver?' Miller said as they cleared up the dinner dishes.

'I know I was taking a risk, but he used psychology on me. He got to the mother in me. All he wanted was to see his little girl.'

Miller switched the dishwasher on. 'And she cottoned on to you right away and called the police.' He laughed. 'She certainly is a smart one.'

'That was my fault; I forgot that she might have seen his face in the papers. Obviously, she knew he was out, but he assumed that she wouldn't recognise him.'

'Hopefully, she can be recruited into the force one day if she's that smart.'

'You know, this case would have been so much easier if that had been Becky McIver they found, instead of Adele Mason.'

'Well, tests confirmed it, as well as dental records, so we have to play the hand we're dealt.'

'I know.' The walked through to the living room. Emma was in her room playing while Annie was in her cot in her bedroom. 'Jack and Samantha have been great helping us with the girls.'

'I know. Your mum and dad, too. Neil is a superb grandfather.'

'He loves them both.' They sat down. 'Want to watch some TV?'

'Sure. Put something on. I'll be there in a minute.' He walked out of the living room to get the sheet of paper Sergeant Hooligan had given him regarding the fingerprint results.

'I know we said we wouldn't bring work home, but I just wanted to have a look at this sheet.'

'Okay.' Kim channel-hopped while Miller took out the sheet and read through the names that had been identified from the fingerprints. They were McIver and other people who were related to Becky, including her sister Dee. And the young people who had found Adele, including Josh Riley.

The list showed not only who the prints belonged to but where the prints were found.

He sat up.

'What's wrong?' Kim asked. 'I can change the channel.'

'No, it's not that.' He told her what he was thinking then stood up and got his coat and grabbed his car keys.

'I'll check in later.'

'Okay, honey. Stay safe.'

THIRTY-TWO

'Now, what delights are you going to shower me with?' Kate Murphy asked Andy Watt.

'Luckily for you, Maggie Parks taught me a couple of things.'

'She's a woman of many talents.'

'She would have to be to live with Paddy Gibb. He's a very demanding man, I hear.'

She pulled away from him, laughing. 'I'll set the table while you dish up the food.'

The doorbell rang. 'Who could this be?' Kate said with a worried look on her face.

'Try checking – that's what the entry phone's there for,' Andy said, stepping out of reach of another slap.

The video entry phone showed Frank Miller standing outside.

'Come on up, Frank,' Kate said, buzzing him in.

'I'm sorry to disturb you,' he said after they let him in. 'Oh, God, you're about to eat. I'm sorry. I can call Steffi Walker. I did try your phone, Andy, but it went to voicemail.'

'Sorry, boss, I had it on silent. But what's up anyway?'

Miller told him.

Kate put a hand on Andy's arm. 'You go with Frank. I can heat the dinner up when you get home.'

'If you're sure?'

'Go.' She kissed him goodbye and the two detectives left.

'Sorry to do this to you, pal,' Miller said as they got into his Audi, 'but I don't think it can wait.' He told him where they were going.

'Don't worry about it. I told you to always call if you need me.'

Miller turned the car around and headed up Holyrood Road. 'I can see you're happy with Kate, pal. I'm happy for you.'

'Cheers, Frank. We both make each other happy. And before you say anything, yes, I learned a lesson after Jean.'

'How is she doing?'

'She's better now. Her son is still an arsehole and always will be, but as long as she's with Molloy, I think he'll toe the line.'

'I called Paddy to let him know what was going on, and he wants us to pick him up,' Miller said, heading down to Broughton first.

Maggie Parks came up the stairs from the basement level with Gibb and leaned into the car when Watt wound the window down.

'Don't you be a stranger, Andy Watt. We can still have game night. And bring Kate with you. I'm moving in permanently with Paddy so you can come round anytime.' She stood up. 'Isn't that right, Paddy?'

'Sure. He can come round every February twenty-ninth.'

'Don't listen to him, Andy.' She leaned back down. 'I'm going to miss you being here.'

'I'll still see you at work. And yes, we'll come round. If only to annoy the wee Irishman.'

Maggie laughed and leaned in to kiss him on the cheek.

'I'll be back soon to get the rest of my stuff.'

'Anytime.'

Watt wound the window up as Gibb got in the back.

'See? Why can't you be nice like her?' Watt said as Miller drove away.

'Being Irish, I have more Irish blood in me than she does.'

'What's that got to do with it?' Miller said.

'How long have you known me, Miller? Have you even known me to be pleasant when being pleasant isn't called for?'

'That's true. Can I come to game night as well?'

'We've graduated from tiddlywinks, so it's above your level.'

They drove to South Gyle and stopped at Dee Raeburn's house. She was surprised to see them.

'Haven't you grilled me enough, detectives?' she said, her face full of anger. It was dark and windy and she pulled her cardigan tighter around herself.

'We need to talk to you about something, Mrs Raeburn.'

She looked at them for a moment, as if they were vacuum cleaner salesmen and she was deciding if she needed a new one or not.

'It's important,' Watt said.

'We're looking for your help,' Gibb said.

She stood back and let them in. They stood around in the hallway until they were directed into the living room.

'I have to say, I'm not impressed, you hauling me into the station and giving me the third degree.'

'You want us to catch the person who harmed your sister, don't you?' Gibb said, getting irritated.

'She's not officially dead, is she?' Dee's lip quivered.

'No, but if somebody has harmed her, we want to catch them.'

'You think Gus is innocent, don't you?' She sat down, while the men remained standing.

'We're keeping an open mind, but if somebody else did harm Becky, wouldn't you want the right person in prison?'

'Of course.'

'That's why we need your help,' Miller said. 'We want to speak to Josh.'

'Josh?' She jumped out of her seat. 'What's he got to do with it?'

'We're hoping he'll help us,' Watt said.

'How can he help you?'

'We can't discuss that, but we think he might have information for us. He just doesn't know it yet. Can you tell us where he is?'

'He's out with his friends again.'

'Ben Robertson?' Miller said.

'Yes. Ben and his friend. I've known them for years, and although they're alright, I just wish Josh wouldn't hang out with them. But what can I do? He's an adult after all, and I should be thankful he doesn't drink or do drugs.'

'He's autistic, isn't he?' Watt said.

'He has Asperger's Syndrome. That's where people make the mistake. Josh can be awkward in social situations, but he's intelligent. He can drive, do normal things, but he's not so good at meeting new people. That's why he finds it hard to get a job. And he wants to stay here most of the time.'

'Did he know Adele?' Gibb asked.

'Yes. She was his best friend. They did everything together. As friends, mind. There wasn't any nonsense going on. He was so upset when she just took off. Now we know what really happened to her.' Her eyes opened wide. 'You don't think...?'

'We don't think anything right now,' Gibb replied, a little too quickly.

'Do you know where they were going?' Miller asked.

'To the quarry. Back to that bunker.'

THIRTY-THREE

'We want you to be in this video, Josh,' Cara Robertson said, putting her arm around Josh's shoulders after they got out of the car.

'Where's Ben?'

'He's with Marty. They went ahead and got the camera gear up and running. You do want to be in the film, don't you?'

'Yes. I like you and Ben and Marty. You're my best friends.'

'And we've been friends for a long time.'

They took torches out and headed over to the entrance. They had permission to film here at night; the project manager had given them a key to the padlock that locked the door.

Inside, their flashlights shone around, picking out graffiti and the smell of decay.

'Where are they?' Josh said, looking around the stone corridors.

'Not far. Let's go up this way.'

They walked further in and down a short corridor then through a doorway.

'This is where it ends, Josh.'

'What do you mean?' He stepped back from her.

'I mean, I'm going to make it look like an accident. You know too much, Josh. If you hadn't come along the other day, if you hadn't found Adele, we wouldn't be here right now.'

Cara was fast. Lithe as a cat, she was on top of Josh before he knew what was happening.

They each dropped their flashlights

He screamed loudly, trying to ward off her blows, but one connected with his face, smacking his nose. Blood spurted out, and Cara made a face and stepped back. Then she stepped sideways and rushed Josh again. He screamed once more. He knew he couldn't hit a girl.

Cara pushed him against the old rusted railings, the light from the flashlights making the scene surreal.

'Help! Help me!' Josh shouted as Cara tried to lift him.

'There's no one here to help you,' she screamed at him.

'I wouldn't be so sure,' Gibb said from the doorway,

shining his light into her eyes. As she let Josh go and put a hand up to her face, Miller and Watt rushed her, pinning her against the wall.

Then Watt handcuffed her.

'Get your hands off me!' she said, squirming.

'You okay?' Gibb asked Josh.

'She killed Adele,' he said. 'She made me help her a long time ago.'

'Shut up, you fool,' Cara said.

'Is that why you tried to kill him just now?' Miller said. 'Because of what he knew?'

Her shoulders slumped. 'Yes.' The fight had gone out of her. 'It was all Ben's fault; if he hadn't wanted to come in here filming, Josh wouldn't have gone to where Adele was.'

'Josh knew where she was hidden,' Gibb said.

'Yes. I was trying to get the others to film in a different part, but they kept following Josh.'

'That's why we watched the film,' Miller said. 'Josh said, *Look what I have*, not *Look what I found*. Subtle difference with a big meaning.'

'He was happy he was going to see his beloved friend again. I thought he would have avoided her like the plague, since he had helped put her there, but it was like he was going to be friends with her,' Cara said. 'But how did you know we were here?'

'Josh's print was on the back of the watch Adele

had in her inside pocket. He would have had to move her corpse to get to it, but she hadn't been disturbed. So that meant he had touched it *before* she was found.'

'For God's sake.'

'Come on, let's get out of here,' Gibb said. 'Andy, call for a wagon and an ambulance.'

Watt took his phone out. 'I'll wait until we're outside.'

When they reached the cars, Miller kept a tight grip on Cara. 'Why did you kill Adele?'

'Despite what Josh says, that's not what happened. Adele came round to my boyfriend's apartment, wanting him to take her back. He refused and a fight broke out. Adele told me my boyfriend had killed a woman years ago. Now she was going to report him for killing this woman. So neither of us would have him anymore. He got angry and killed Adele. He couldn't risk her going to the police. After she was lying dead in his bathroom, I had Josh come round and help me move her.'

'Who was the woman he supposedly killed years before?' Gibb said.

'The woman whose name has been in the paper: Becky McIver.'

'Did he admit to you that he killed Becky?'

'Yes. Then he said, back when he was Adele's

boyfriend, he'd asked her to go and steal a watch and some jewellery that was in McIver's house.'

Miller looked at Gibb. 'Just what McIver said; he thought Becky came back and took it. Turns out Adele Mason went in and took it.'

'Why would he want her to go and take it?'

Cara smiled. 'Easy; he wanted it to look like Becky simply walked out. And it worked, didn't it? You arrested her husband.'

'Where did he kill her?'

'He killed Becky in her house in Trinity. The kids weren't around but Adele had a key and they had used the house to screw in. Becky caught them and she was pissed off because she was screwing him too. She had fallen in love with him. She was going to tell his then wife, so my boyfriend killed her.'

'Who is this guy?' Gibb asked.

'Why should I tell you?'

'Here's the thing,' Gibb said, taking a step closer. 'He's going to sit back and let you take the fall for it. And while you're rotting in prison, he's going to go out and get another young woman to be his girlfriend. How will you feel then?'

Her whole demeanour changed after she thought about it. 'We also rob houses,' she said, gritting her teeth in anger.

'Rob houses?' Gibb said.

'Yes. Just for the hell of it. Then we sell the stuff. Normally, we get my brother and Marty Williams to befriend divorced women at a singles club, ones who appear to have money. Weeks later, when the women trust them, the boys are in the bar with them and we go and rob their house.'

'Again, he's going to walk away scot-free while you're behind bars. Unless you tell us his name.'

Gibb could see the anger appearing on her face. Then she told them the name. *Lord Snooty.*

THIRTY-FOUR

'Here's to us, ladies,' Robert Molloy said, and he froze for a second as the doorbell rang. 'I wonder who this is?' He left the room to answer it.

They were in the formal dining room next door to the living room.

'This steak looks fantastic,' the blonde said.

'I have a feeling we're not going to be able to enjoy it.' The brunette looked disappointed.

They heard voices at the door and Molloy came back in with Adam Melrose. The younger man was carrying a holdall, which he put on the floor.

'Ladies, this is my girlfriend's son, Adam. You want a piece of steak?' he asked Melrose as he sat down.

'No thanks, I'm not staying long.'

'What can I do for you?'

The two young women looked at Melrose.

'You just couldn't fucking help yourself, could you?'

Molloy's smile dropped. 'What did you say?' He made to stand up but Melrose brought a kitchen knife from inside his coat pocket.

'My mother's in hospital, and you have two fucking tarts round for a quick bite to eat then upstairs for a good time. I'm surprised you think your heart is strong enough.'

'This is not what you think.'

Melrose laughed, tilting his head back for a second. 'Don't they always say that? Usually when they've got their trousers round their ankles, but all the same. I think that's exactly what it is.'

'You're wrong,' the blonde woman said.

'Shut your hole, bitch!' he said, pointing the knife in her direction.

'Take it easy, Adam,' the brunette said.

'What, you speak as well? I bet he didn't hire you for your eloquence though.'

'What's your problem?' Molloy said. 'Didn't we work things out?'

Melrose laughed again. 'Sort things out? Is that what you fucking call it? You beat me and held a gun to my head!'

'Gun? Jesus, I don't own a gun. You told me you fell down some steps.'

The laughter stopped. 'Oh, I see; witnesses. You don't want to admit to having a gun in front of your two whores.'

'Put the knife away, Adam,' Molloy said.

'What? You don't think I've got it in me? I fucking killed Josh McIver's wife six years ago. She thought we were exclusive and took a tantrum when she caught me sleeping with the babysitter, Adele Mason. I had been sleeping with both of them, but Becky wanted me to leave my wife. When she caught me and Adele, she went berserk. I hit the bitch. She died.'

'I don't believe you. It's been all over the papers,' the blonde said. 'Gus McIver killed his wife then tried to make it look like she disappeared.'

'Was I even fucking talking to you?' He pointed the knife in her direction again. 'The papers know nothing. I was the one who killed her.'

'No you didn't,' Molloy said. 'You haven't got it in you.'

Melrose laughed. 'I killed her. That would have been the end of it, but six months ago, Adele wanted me back. I told her no, I had a new girlfriend. She started to get stroppy, then she threatened to go to the police. So I killed Adele, and my girlfriend along with Josh Riley, dumped her in the old bunker in Corstorphine Hill.'

'Who's your girlfriend?' Molloy asked. 'Give me

her number and I'll give her a call. See if she can corroborate your story. Then I might believe you.'

'Shut your fucking mouth, Molloy. You think you're the hard bastard who slaps people about? I'm the crazy one here.'

'Adele was discovered. You couldn't have hidden her that well,' blondie said.

'You know, I'm sick of you bitches poking your noses in. I'm talking to him, so shut it.' He looked at Molloy. 'My girlfriend is Cara. Her stupid brother wanted to film in that place and they took that daft bastard along. Cara knew it was a bad idea because Josh had already helped dump Adele. And the dafty had to go running to her.'

'And Adele had kept Becky McIver's watch. It was in the papers,' added brunette.

'That's right. So now Josh is going to have an accident. Cara's getting rid of the bastard. Just after I take care of you three. Pity, Molloy. It was only going to be you, but you brought these slags round. Now you're all going to get it and I'm going to set fire to this dump and burn it to the ground.'

He'd reached down to the holdall to bring out the can of petrol when blondie got up from her chair, grabbed the candelabra from the table and swung it at Melrose. He saw it coming and put up an arm which received the full force of the candelabra. The brunette was right behind her but she had brought out an extendable baton and smacked it over Melrose's shoulder.

The front door crashed open just as Steffi Walker and Julie Stott were rolling Melrose over.

Andy Watt and Frank Miller ran in, Watt kicking Melrose hard between the legs as the man lay on his front.

All the fight went out of him as he screamed.

Molloy stood up and put the steak knife he had grabbed back on the table.

'You took your time, Miller,' he said.

'Luckily for you, two of my finest sergeants were able to come at short notice,' he replied, nodding to the two women.

'Hey, I'm right here,' Watt said.

'I'm kidding, I'm kidding,' Molloy said. 'You and Andy are a sight for sore eyes. But as you can see, the ladies had it well in hand. And if he'd got close to me, I would—'

Watt put a finger to his lips and made a sign that the conversation was being recorded.

'—have wrestled with him until the ladies could get the better of him.'

Uniforms rushed in after Miller had stuck his head out into the hall and waved for them to come in.

'I'm sure Cara Robertson is going to sing like a bird,' blondie, aka Steffi Walker said.

'She already is. DCI Gibb escorted her to the station.'

Molloy poured himself a drink from the drinks cabinet. 'That little bastard. Jean is going to be devastated.'

'He always hated me too, if it makes you feel better,' Watt said.

'It doesn't, but cheers anyway.' He drank more whisky. 'He was going to kill us and then burn the place down. That would have gotten me out of his hair once and for all.'

'What he said about the gun...?' Julie Stott said.

'It was all pish, coming from a mad man. Gun indeed. He probably got a slap from somebody.'

'That's what I thought.'

'Where are your staff?' Miller asked.

'After you called me, I told them to go out for the evening. I wasn't going to put them at risk. They're away to the pictures or something. My driver has them so they're safe.'

'That took guts, staying here when you knew Melrose could appear at any moment.'

'Just as well that Cara lassie told you. But I wonder what those younger women saw in him? And how did he know to send Adele Mason back into the house to get that jewellery?' Molloy finished the whisky.

'Hopefully, he'll tell us.' Miller turned to Steffi. 'You made sure the wire you're wearing is working properly?'

'Yes, it was fine.'

'Yours too, Julie?'

'Yes.'

Molloy smiled. 'Since we didn't get to finish our dinner, please allow me and Jean to treat you one night.'

'Kind offer, but no thanks,' Miller said.

'Unless you've changed your name to Julie or Steffi recently, that invitation didn't include you, Miller.'

'We'll need a statement from you.'

'I'll be along to the station tomorrow. Just don't say anything to Michael about this.'

'Dad! Dad!' They heard Michael Molloy shout as he came rushing into the house.

'Too late,' Miller said.

THIRTY-FIVE

It was cold but bracing as Miller stood at the edge of Inverleith Pond, throwing bread to the ducks with his stepdaughter. Kim sat on a bench with Annie in her pram.

'Here, you take the last few pieces. Don't go too close to the edge,' he said to Emma, then he walked back to the bench and sat down next to his wife.

'Those two detectives were so brave,' she said.

'Julie and Steffi are two of the finest on my team.'

'And Melrose talked?'

'Yes, he did.'

'And my mother is talking to the Lord Advocate now, to have all charges dropped against Gus McIver. Dee, his sister-in-law is going to help him rehabilitate.'

'I still can't believe it was Melrose. He killed that poor woman. Then he asked Adele to go and steal the watch and jewellery to make it look like Becky had simply walked out.'

'Then six years later he has the nerve to murder the girl who helped bury Becky and steal the jewellery. He planted it on her, so if she was ever found, it would implicate her in Becky's disappearance,' Kim said.

Miller nodded. 'Being an advocate, he saw the crime scene photos that showed the watch on the dresser. He was the one who ordered more photos taken. He wasn't the QC representing McIver, but the firm was. So Melrose knew all about McIver's life and he knew the inside of the house.'

'Clyde Mason isn't going to be too happy finding out what his daughter was involved in back then.'

'When is Melrose going to take you to where he buried Becky?'

'He's not.'

Kim looked at him suddenly. 'Why not? He said he would.'

Miller shrugged. 'Now he's not. Maybe we'll never find out.'

'Jean Melrose is going to need all the support she can get. She's still in the Royal. But we'll make sure she's okay. And Molloy will spare no expense,' Kim said and reached over and squeezed his hand. 'I love you, Frank Miller.'

'Love you too.'

THIRTY-SIX

Andy Watt stood six feet away from the stone-cold killer and didn't blink.

'She doesn't know you're here,' Jill White said, standing next to him.

'I know.'

They were in the observation room again, looking in at Eve Ross as she sat at a table. Then quietly and without fuss, Eve stood up and walked over to the large mirror in the room and stood before it.

Andy Watt knew she couldn't see him but it still made the hairs on the back of his neck stand up.

Then Eve put her face closer to the glass, raised her right hand and put it against the mirror, palm facing Watt.

He hesitated for a moment then raised his left hand and put it against the glass, against Eve's palm.

Jill White left the room.

Andy Watt stood like that for no more than a minute. 'Goodbye, Eve,' he said and walked out of the room.

AFTERWORD

I want to mention again, that my characters have opinions that are not necessarily mine. This book is fiction, and does not represent me in any way, shape or form.

I would like to take this opportunity to thank my advance reading team.

Thank you to my wife Debbie, who works away in the background. My daughters, Stephanie and Samantha.

If I can ask you to please leave an honest review on Amazon or Goodreads, that would be fantastic. Every review counts, and a few minutes out of your day will help an author like me to be able to continue writing.

And a big thank you to you, the reader, for joining me on this outing. Without you, it's all for nothing.

All the best my friends.

John Carson
New York
March 2019

ABOUT THE AUTHOR

John Carson is originally from Edinburgh, Scotland, but now lives with his wife and family in New York State. And two dogs. And four cats.

www.johncarsonauthor.com

Printed in Great Britain
by Amazon